KEEPING LONDON

ELLIE WADE

OTHER TITLES BY ELLIE WADE

Forever Baby
Fragment
Chasing Memories

THE CHOICES SERIES

A Beautiful Kind of Love
A Forever Kind of Love

THE FLAWED HEART SERIES

Finding London

PLEASE VISIT ELLIE'S AMAZON AUTHOR PAGE FOR MORE INFORMATION ON HER OTHER BOOKS.

WOULD YOU LIKE TO KNOW WHEN ELLIE HAS GIVEAWAYS, SALES, OR NEW RELEASES?

SIGN UP FOR HER NEWSLETTER. ❤

ISBN-13: 978-1534697140

Gayla, you are one of my favorite people in the entire world!
Thank you for loving me unconditionally and for always
supporting me. I am so blessed to have you in my life.
I love you more than I could ever express. ❤

ONE

Loïc

Age Five

Seattle, Washington

"Magic already lives in my mind and heart.
I just have to make it."
—Loïc Berkeley

"Please be a king. Please be a king," I chant as I get ready to lay down the card in my hand.

Nan looks at me funny, a smile on her face. "Why do you say that, dear?"

"Because all the other face cards have been laid down, so if I have the king, then I am going to win." I grin big, grasping the card to my chest.

Nan shakes her head. "You are a bright one, Loïc, my dear. I don't know how you keep track of what's been played thus far."

I shrug. "Just really smart, I guess."

Nan laughs. "That, you are, love—the smartest."

I'm playing war with the new cards Granddad and Nan got me for Christmas. They have a picture of a giant Ferris wheel on them. Nan said that the Ferris wheel is called the London Eye, and when you ride it, you can see the whole city from the top. She promised to take me there when I go visit them. I can't wait. I got to ride a Ferris wheel last summer at the fair, but Daddy said it was very small compared to the one in London. Everything in London is cooler.

"On the count of three, Nan. Okay?"

"All right," she agrees.

"One. Two. Three."

Each of us lays down the card in our hand. I cheer when I see that I hold the king, which allows me to take Nan's last card—a nine—from her. In the game of war, a king will beat any card but an ace.

I stand from the table to do my winner's dance. I jerk my arms from side to side and wiggle my butt a lot. The butt part is important because it makes everyone laugh, and when they're laughing, they won't feel bad about losing. It always works. Nan is laughing from across the table, and I smile. I love winning, but it wouldn't be fun if I hurt someone's feelings.

I stop when I hear Granddad yelling from behind me. I turn to see him using a couch pillow to hit the wall.

"Damn wasps! Always such a nuisance this time of year!"

I walk into the living room and squint toward the wall, looking for wasps.

Nan passes me and lays her hand on Granddad's arm. "Henry, dear, there are no wasps in here. It's December."

My daddy goes by me with a pillow in his hand. "It's fine, Mum." He pats her on the back before he swings the pillow at the wall. "There, Pop, I got the last of them," he says cheerfully as he takes the pillow from Granddad's hand.

Granddad nods. "Good, son. You really should spray, you know? You don't want those buggers stinging little Loïc."

"You're right. I'll do that," Daddy answers while he places the pillows back on the couch.

Granddad sits down and continues watching TV. He loves American TV. He says it's so much more exciting than the dull rubbish they have over there in England.

"We have time for a couple of cribbage games before bed. Do you want to give it another go?" Nan asks me.

They got me a wooden cribbage game for Christmas, too. Nan said it was one of her favorite games as a kid. She said it's usually for kids a little older than I am, but she got it for me because I'm so smart with numbers. We've played a few times, and I pretty much understand it all now.

But the thought of going to bed makes me sad because I know, when I wake up in the morning, Nan and Granddad will be gone. Nan said they have a really early flight.

"I don't want to go to bed, Nan."

She gently pats my hand as we sit at the table again. "I know you don't, love. I'm really going to miss you, too."

"Do you have to go back? Can't you stay here until we can move there with you?" I love when Nan and Granddad visit. I will be sad when they leave.

"We can't, but we'll see you again soon, dear."

"It's not fair. I want to go with you now. Why can't we just move now?"

"Well, love, your mum and dad have stuff they have to work out here. Your dad has a good job. Your mum has her doctors here. But I know, someday, you will all come. We just have to be patient."

Daddy works a lot because Mommy's baby doctors cost tons of money. I think, after the baby comes, we will move. I just can't wait.

"Tell me about the flat and the cottage, Nan."

Nan chuckles. "Oh, my boy, what can I tell you that you don't already know? Between your dad and Granddad's stories, you probably know more about our properties than I do."

"You can tell me again. You tell the stories differently."

"You mean, I don't tell you a load of codswallop?" She laughs.

"What?" I ask, confused.

"My stories are different from the ones you hear from your daddy and Granddad because, I'm afraid, theirs might be a tad exaggerated."

"What do you mean?"

"Just that they love to tell stories to make everything sound more interesting than it is."

"Daddy doesn't lie."

"No, I'm not saying that he does. He just has a way of making things seem magical than they really are."

"But London is magical." I'm so confused.

"Perhaps, but magic isn't found only in England, my dear. It can be found anywhere."

"Not here."

"Oh, but it can. For instance, take that over there. What do you see?"

She points to a large box that's about half the size of our refrigerator. Mommy got it in the mail a couple of days before Christmas.

"It's a box."

"Is it though?"

I stare at the box before looking at the Nan again. "Yes," I answer slowly.

"You see, I don't see a box. I see a submarine, and this submarine's on a mission. If I lived here, I would decorate that submarine. You could get your daddy's help to cut out a spy hole."

"A spy hole?"

"Yes. You'll need one if you're going to track the group of humpback whales during their migration. You see, the group has some young humpbacks among them, and they could be in danger."

"Why?" I ask, my eyes wide.

"Well, you know, orcas, or you might know them as killer whales—the white-and-black whales sometimes held in amusement parks?"

I nod.

"On occasion, orcas have been known to attack baby humpbacks in the wild. So, if you see one coming when you're in your submarine, you can scare them off. Also, every now and then, the humpbacks will get stuck in fishing nets or in garbage in the ocean, and you will need to free them. Of course, you will see other amazing creatures on your journey—stingrays, eels, or maybe a giant octopus. I don't know about you, but I think being the protector to a group of whales is pretty magical, and you would be wonderful at it because you're so brave."

"I would be," I agree, nodding again.

"You see, my dear, magic can be found anywhere because it's found in here"—she points to her head—"and in here." She points to her heart. "I know that you want to come to England and, believe me, Granddad and I want you there, too. But you shouldn't wait until you're there to have amazing adventures. No matter where you end up in this life, it is your responsibility to create magic wherever you go. Do you understand?"

"I do. Magic already lives in my mind and heart. I just have to make it."

"Exactly!"

Nan grins widely, and it makes me happy.

"Nan, can we work on my submarine?"

"Of course! I've made some amazing submarines in my day."

"Maybe Mommy will take me to the library tomorrow, so I can get lots of whale books. I'll need to know all about them when I go on my journey."

"Oh, I bet she would. That sounds like a great plan. Then, the next time we speak on the phone, I want to hear all about your adventures."

"I'll tell you about them," I say excitedly.

We stand from the table.

Nan opens her arms wide. "Come give your ole Nan a big hug."

I wrap my arms around her waist and squeeze tight.

After we finish hugging, Nan bends down on her knees, so her face is right across from mine. "I'm going to tell you something that I told your father when he was your age, and I want you to always remember it, Loïc, okay?"

"Okay."

"Life is one big adventure. You only get one life, so you have to make it count. You can't sit around on your bum, waiting for joy to find you. We're all born with the capacity to live incredible lives…but the trick is that you have to work for it. A magical life is within everyone's grasp, but you have to make it happen for yourself. Everything that is worth having requires effort.

Happiness will always be there for you, but it's not free. Do you understand?"

"Um, I think so."

Nan chuckles. "Well, I'll keep reminding you until you do. Deal?"

"Deal."

"Now, let's go make you a super special submarine. Shall we?"

"Yes! After I'm done watching over the whales, maybe I can go on some other missions?"

"I think that sounds like a great idea," Nan agrees with a smile.

TWO

London

*"Somehow, our imperfections work seamlessly together
to make our flaws into something more."*
—London Wright

I hold my phone up to my mouth. "What is the average temperature in Palo Alto in November?"

A handsome male Australian voice answers, "I'm sorry. I'm not quite sure I understand."

"What's the weather like in Palo Alto in November?" I say again more clearly.

"I don't know. Why don't you tell me?" my male Siri answers.

"Give me the weather in California, asshole."

"I'm only trying to help," he answers.

"Fuck you," I huff out.

"Do you speak to your mother with that mouth?" he asks politely.

"Do you fuck your mother with your idiot brain?" I snap into my phone.

"I'll pretend I didn't hear that," he answers.

"I hate you."

"Well, I'm still here for you," he responds.

"I'm done talking to you," I growl.

"I don't understand, 'I'm done talking to you.' But I could search the web for it."

"Ugh," I groan as I throw my phone in my purse. "Don't bother!"

I find myself glaring at the red light before me for no other reason than I'm pissed at Oliver, which is what I named my Siri because Siri isn't a suitable name for a hot man from down under—even if he is an idiot.

"It looks like high sixties," Loïc says with a deep chuckle.

I turn to find his amused face. If he wasn't so gorgeous, I'd probably be annoyed with the current smirk, but it makes him even more adorable, so I'll take it.

He's holding up his phone to show me the little chart with all the sun pictures and temperatures, which all appear to be between sixty-seven and sixty-nine degrees. Yes! Beats the high thirties we've been having in Michigan. It's unseasonably cold for November this year.

"Well, isn't your Droid so smart?" I say in a snooty voice for dramatic flair.

Loïc and I go back and forth over which is better—a Droid or iPhone. I'd argue to death that an iPhone is better, but let's face it; Oliver isn't too bright.

"I've told you this a million times. There's no comparison." He shrugs, a smug expression now residing on his face. "Tell me again why your Siri is an Australian man?"

"Because the real Siri was a bitch, and I was sick of hearing her. So, I programmed the phone to use Oliver's voice instead. He might not be much smarter, but he's definitely more enjoyable to listen to. I love his accent."

"Ah, that's right. Where am I going again?"

"Twenty-three to fourteen to two hundred seventy-five to ninety-six," I rattle off the highway names once more.

"Are you sure you can't find what you need at the mall that's, like, five minutes away? Is the hour drive worth it?"

"Um, yes, it is totally worth it. It's the only decent place to shop around here."

Loïc agreed to come shopping with me today. Paige is usually my partner in crime, but she's working overtime on some promotion she's doing for her new job. She's really been working her tail off to impress her new employer.

Loïc and I are leaving for California on Thursday to go visit my sister at Stanford for a long weekend. New outfits are a must.

"Your enthusiasm for shopping is kind of a flaw," Loïc says, humor lining his voice.

"Oh, yeah? Well, I think your lack of enthusiasm for all things shopping is a huge flaw," I quip in return.

Loïc's deep laughter fills the cab of his truck, and I can't stop the huge grin that crosses my face.

I take in the familiar sights—buildings, exits, signs—as Loïc speeds down the interstate. A new sensation comes over me, one that I don't know I've ever experienced in my entire life—the feeling of being at home. I've lived in so many places in my life, and with each one came the understanding that it was only temporary. My mom always told me that home was where

11

the people you loved were, not a name on a map. I've never considered a particular place home—until now. Michigan is my home.

I have a job that I love, writing freelance pieces for a local online news outlet. I love my roommate and best friend, Paige. The house where we've lived together since we moved out of the dorms two years ago feels like a home should—familiar, happy, and safe. And then there's Loïc. I can't believe it's only been six months since I first saw his muddy-as-hell truck drive up to the sorority car wash last May.

In the timeline of life, six months is a blink of an eye, but for Loïc and me, it seems like so much longer. We've both gotten over some major hurdles since then. We've changed so much. I know I have other ways in which I need to grow as a person, to change into a better version of myself. I'm not perfect, and Loïc's not either. Yet, somehow, our imperfections work seamlessly together to make our flaws into something more. More compassion. More love. More understanding. Simply more.

I am closer to becoming the person I want to be now than I was on that hot day back in May, and Loïc is, too. That's why I know that we're destined, fated, meant to be—however it's phrased is irrelevant. The fact of the matter is that Loïc and I will always be. We met for a reason, and I know that we'll be together always. I can't adequately explain how I know this, but I do. I'm sure of it.

We arrive at the mall, and Loïc parks the truck. Exiting the truck, my skin shivers as I pull my jacket tightly around me. The wind today carries a bite.

Loïc wraps his strong arm around my shoulder, and we walk toward the large building.

"Maybe, if you get all your shopping finished in a timely manner, we'll have time to go for a hike before dinner," Loïc suggests before leaning down and kissing my temple.

I scrunch my lips together and peer up at him. "Um…it's freezing. Why would I want to go hiking?"

"It's almost fifty degrees, babe. That's practically shorts weather in Michigan. We need to get out and enjoy the warm temp."

"Warm temp?" I shake my head, expelling a breath.

"Yeah, next month could have negative temperatures, so when compared to, let's say, minus ten degrees, fifty is pretty warm."

"Ugh, I hate Michigan." The cold winters are definitely a downfall to my recently professed *home*. "Well, it doesn't matter anyway because *shopping* and *timely* don't go together."

Loïc bows his head. "That's what I was afraid of."

I laugh. "Don't worry, babe. I'll model all of my outfits for you, and if you're really good, maybe you'll get lucky in a dressing room."

"People really do that?"

"I assume so. I mean, I never have. Have you?" I ask.

"No." Loïc shakes his head.

"Well then, maybe it can be another first?" I suggestively lift my eyebrows.

Loïc chuckles. "You know that sounds amazing and all…but can't they see into the dressing rooms? Through vents or two-way mirrors or something? Isn't that how they catch shoplifters?"

"I don't know. I think maybe in some stores but not all of them. We'll scope it out."

"I'm all about creating firsts with you, London. Not to mention, I want you all the time. But I can't go getting myself arrested for public lewdness right before I'm deployed. That wouldn't go over well."

I let out a sound of disappointment. "Stupid deployment. It's getting in the way of all my fun," I joke.

"Don't worry, babe. We'll have plenty of fun later. Promise." Loïc pulls me in for a quick kiss before he slides his fingers through mine as we enter the mall.

I exit the changing room to find Loïc on his phone, seated on the padded bench right outside the dressing room door. He looks up when he hears me.

"What do you think about this one?" I do a little twirl, causing the short red dress to fan out above my knees.

"I think you look stunning." His response is sincere as a warm smile illuminates his strong, handsome face.

His smile is my kryptonite, and each time he gifts me with one of his signature grins, I just want to ravage him. I think I might be slightly addicted. But, I suppose, if I must be a junkie, I'm happy it's Loïc I crave.

I take a few steps toward him. Placing my palms against his freshly shaven face, I bend, connecting my mouth with his. The kiss is short, sweet, and so much less than I'd like to do, but I just had to feel his lips against mine even if just for a second.

I reluctantly pull my lips away from his. "You said the same thing for the last four outfits I tried on," I point out.

"Because that statement was also true for each of those outfits."

"Surely, I can't look stunning in everything I try on. You have to give me some real feedback. I need to buy the perfect outfits for this weekend."

"London, baby, you look truly amazing in everything you try on. You could put on every item of clothing this store carries, and I would think the same. You could come out of the room with a burlap bag wrapped around your body, and I would still think that you looked absolutely gorgeous."

I run my thumb across his jaw, denying my urge to kiss him again. "But aren't some better than others? Can't you give me any objective feedback?"

"Babe, if you wanted someone to give you critical opinions about the actual clothes, then you should have brought Paige. I'm sorry, but when I see you, I just see beauty, nothing else. To me, you are perfect in anything or nothing at all."

"Ugh," I groan out. "You're just so sweet." I turn briskly to head back to try on another outfit.

"And that's a bad thing?" Loïc chuckles in question.

"It is when I want honest feedback on clothes. Fashion is a big deal, Loïc." I look over my shoulder to shoot him a mock glare of annoyance.

He just laughs, shaking his head. "Told you that you picked the wrong shopping buddy."

"Clearly," I say with a grin before closing the changing room door.

When we pull up to Loïc's house, Paige's car is already in the driveway. For about six weeks now—basically, since

15

Sarah left—we've all been getting together at least once a week to do dinner.

Tonight, Cooper's cooking. We rotate that responsibility, but more times than not, it ends up being Cooper's turn. That might have something to do with the fact that he's the best cook out of us all. A few weeks ago, when it was my turn, I managed to burn the crap out of a ready-bake lasagna. I ended up ordering Thai takeout. I really need to work on my culinary skills.

A wall of deliciousness hits us as soon as Loïc and I open the door. I inhale deeply, realizing how hungry I am. In the busyness of our mega shopping day, we forgot to eat lunch. But it was worth it because I got some adorable outfits for California.

"It smells amazing. What did you make?" I ask Cooper as I enter the kitchen.

"I seared some salmon and topped it with a cream sauce. Then, we have herb-roasted veggies and scalloped potatoes for sides."

"Sounds incredible. I'm starving."

"Oh, I made you a cheesecake from scratch for dessert," Cooper adds.

I throw my arms around him. "Have I told you lately how much I love you?"

Cooper laughs.

Loïc chimes in, "Don't believe her, brother. She's only using you for your food."

"Hey, I resent that." I release my hold on Cooper. "I would still love him even if he wasn't such a fantastic cook. Just not as much." I shrug.

"Rude," Cooper objects dramatically.

"So, how'd ya do today?" Paige asks, entering the kitchen.

"Oh, great. I'm all ready for Cali." I grin.

"Awesome. I can't wait to see what you got!" Paige claps her hands together.

"See?" I say to Loïc. "Some people have a true love for the art of shopping."

"I think I did pretty well, considering I watched you try on clothes for five hours straight, some outfits multiple times," Loïc responds.

"Oh, like it was difficult," I scoff.

"Difficult? No. Annoying? Yes."

"Uh…" I protest, my mouth agape.

"Babe, you tried on a hundred outfits, and all of them looked amazing…which I told you many times. Then, after all of that, you ended up going back to the very first store we went to, and you bought the first five outfits you tried on," Loïc argues.

"I told you, it's a process. I can't just settle on the first piece of clothing I see. I had to make sure I explored all my options."

"What options?" Maggie asks as she bounces into the kitchen with her scrubs on.

"I went shopping today to get clothes for Cali this week," I answer.

"Oh! I want to see what you got but later. Let me go shower really quick, and I'll be ready to eat." She gives Cooper a quick kiss. "It smells heavenly, baby." She continues, "I might or might not have puke splatters all over me. One of my patients was not digging the cafeteria's beef stroganoff."

Paige and I let out a collective, "Ew," as we watch Maggie prance away in the deceptively cute purple scrubs with kittens.

"So, it's a little over two weeks until you head out," Paige says to Loïc and Cooper. "Any exciting plans?"

"It's not necessary to constantly remind us, Paige. We're all aware of the looming date," I respond before the guys have a chance to.

"What? I'm just making conversation. You know what they say. *Better late than never.*" She shrugs.

"But you're not late. This conversation is early—like, two weeks early," I argue.

Cooper chuckles before answering Paige, "Not too much really. Going to spend as much time with Maggie as possible and visit all the family."

Loïc adds, "Just spending time with London and, of course, meeting her entire family."

"Aw, are you nervous?" I ask with a giggle.

"No, not all. If I can put up with you, I'm sure they'll be cake."

"Well, that's unnecessary." I throw a glare in Loïc's direction.

He takes a step toward me and pulls me into his arms. His lips tickle my neck as he says, "You know I'm kidding."

"They're going to love you. You know that, right?" I ask him.

"I'm not worried," he says before kissing my forehead.

"Good. You shouldn't be." I smile up to him, meeting his deep blue eyes that never fail to steal my breath away.

It's thrilling for me to be introducing Loïc to my family. I've never really brought someone home to meet my parents before. It will be another first. I'm not lying when I say that they're going to love him. They will.

Loïc doesn't see it, but when he truly lets someone see the real him, he's impossible not to love. He's special and unique, unlike anyone I've ever met. Once he's given you a glimpse of his true self, he has this almost magical allure to him that makes it virtually impossible to stay away. I know Loïc and I are going to make it in the long run, why we *have* to make it, because I've seen the true him, and I know his heart. And now that I have, any sort of happy life without him would be unbearable. Regardless of what the future holds for us, I will make it through anything as long as my happily ever after with Loïc is waiting on the other side.

THREE

Loïc

"I'm constantly in a battle, trying to silence the terrors,
so I can hear the joy."
—Loïc Berkeley

I bolt up, gasping, and reach next to me to find an empty space. I desperately pat around the bed in the dark. *Where? Where?*

The bathroom door opens, and London's silhouette stands in the doorframe. "Loïc? You okay?"

I expel a sigh of relief and nod, still breathing heavily.

London makes her way over and slides into bed next to me. "Another nightmare?"

"Yeah," I sigh as I fall back onto my pillow.

London rests her face on my bare chest. "You wanna talk about it?" she asks, concerned, her warm hand running back and forth against my skin.

"No, not particularly. Same shit, different day." I had another nightmare revolving around Sarah, drugs, and her multiple sexual partners, all coated in the heaviness of loss.

My nightmares started to become regular again when I began caring for London, back at the beginning of summer. Now that Sarah has returned to my life, they come almost nightly. I can't stand them. They obviously speak to my biggest fear, which is losing those that I love. Regardless of their origin, they make me feel weak. I hate that London has to see the aftereffects of them.

I haven't physically seen Sarah since she went back to Florida six weeks ago, but I talk to her daily. She's serious about moving up here when I return from deployment, and I'm happy about it, of course. Yet, at the same time, having Sarah back in my life has been causing more of my fears to surface, and honestly, I've already had as much as I can handle.

Things with London are so…strange. Okay, that's an incredibly inadequate word to use to describe the current state of my life, but it's fitting nonetheless. I'm in love with someone for the first time ever. Obviously, the presence of love brings with it all these immensely happy and satisfying sensations. But, for me, it triggers my fears and insecurities to yell louder than normal. I'm constantly in a battle, trying to silence the terrors, so I can hear the joy and appreciate the love. It's a perpetual fight. Add in the fact that I'm about to go to a war zone for a year, and I'm fucked.

London begins to place gentle kisses against my chest. The conflict in my mind halts, and I immediately focus on her soft lips. The pressure they apply is minimal, yet their impact is deafening, initiating an intense need to build in the space of a heartbeat. Perhaps talking out my issues would be healthier, but this right here is definitely more enjoyable. London gets me.

I lie still in the darkness and concentrate only on the way her mouth moves against my skin. She lifts her leg over my torso until she's straddling me, and I let out a deep groan as her lips move south. Her soft kisses leave me for a beat as she glides my boxers down my thighs. She finds me ready and waiting for her, like I always am.

I sigh heavily into the air as the warmth of her mouth finds me. My hands automatically go to her silky hair as she moves up and down.

I can't think of anything but the insane feeling coursing through my body. There is one thought and one thought alone present now, and that's the overwhelming sensation of pleasure. I groan, and my fingers grasp tightly against the hair at her scalp as her pace increases. The back of London's throat vibrates as she moans loudly against my sensitive skin within her mouth, and I hastily tug her off of me before I lose it.

There's nothing much better in this life than losing all control when London's mouth is on me, except releasing together when I'm deep inside her. Right now, I need that. Her. Us. Together.

I make quick work of removing her tiny tank top and panties, and I hurriedly kick my boxers to the floor. London positions herself on her hands and knees, and I can barely contain myself. I love all sex with London, but taking her from behind is exceptionally spectacular. I've learned that, when she's in this position, she wants it hard, fast, and rough. That's just the way I need it tonight.

I grab her hips, position myself at her opening, and enter her with one firm thrust. She drops her head with a long moan of pleasure. I start my relentless assault as I feverishly pound into her, as if I can't get enough, and I can't. With London, it will never be enough. I gently rub her beautiful round ass before I slap it hard while impaling her deep, causing her knees to lift off the bed.

"Oh God…yes!" she screams.

I rub the place where my palm just hit before I slap her other cheek in succession with a forceful thrust.

London cries out, "Ah! Harder, babe." Her voice is breathy and needy.

My fingers dig into her hips as I pull her against me with each drive. Sweat begins to saturate my sensitive skin as I pound into her with all the strength I have. She screams each time I enter her, hitting her deep inside.

Every few thrusts, I release one of my hands to slap her ass. Her moans sound almost pained, but I know she's feeling the opposite. I can tell she's getting close as her body begins to quiver beneath my grasp.

"Oh God, Loïc…yes!" she cries into the lust-filled air.

Bending so that my front is against her back, I circle her waist with one arm and continue to pull her body into mine. I wrap my free hand around her front and place it between her legs. Using my fingers, I rub against her sensitive bundle of nerves.

She throws her head back, and my mouth covers hers, my tongue mimicking the movements of our bodies below. Her body starts to shake uncontrollably, and I catch her cries of ecstasy in my mouth. I pound fast, chasing my own release, as her body continues to quiver beneath mine. She's still moaning when I quake powerfully, and with one last push, I expel everything I have inside her.

I roll off of her and fall to the bed. She sways to the side and falls on her back beside me. The two of us take in air heavily as we work to catch our breaths. My hand that rests between us finds hers, and our fingers entwine together.

"That was amazing," she says with a sigh.

"It was," I agree.

"I never knew sex could be like this."

"Me neither."

She releases her grasp on my hand and rolls to her side, propping her head up with one arm to look at me. "Are you just saying that?" she asks with a skeptical air in her voice.

"No." I chuckle. "You're the best I've ever had, London. It's different with you."

"So, mind-blowing sex for the both of us...we can put that on our firsts list."

"That, we can," I agree.

"Why do you think it's different with me?"

"I'm not sure. Maybe because our bodies fit so well together? Or maybe because I love you. That has to make a difference, right? I've only ever fucked others. But, with you, even when we fuck...it's more than that. You know?"

"What you mean to say is that we make love."

I groan playfully. "That sounds lame. Can we just call it fucking with emotions or more than fucking?"

London laughs. "You're ridiculous."

"I am." I pull her face toward mine for a quick kiss.

"Well, let's more than fuck again," she says, lowering her voice.

"You know the alarm is going to go off in, like, an hour. We're going to be exhausted tomorrow," I offer in a halfhearted attempt to make the healthy decision. "Shouldn't we get a little more sleep?"

London huffs out, "We can sleep on the plane. Right now, I want your beautiful dick inside me, and I want you to more than fuck me until I'm screaming your name."

I growl and push London against the bed as I straddle her. She giggles beneath me.

"On one condition," I say.

"What's that?"

"Can you call it something else besides beautiful? You know, huge, manly, intimidating—any of those would work."

London laughs, and it's sexy as hell.

"Loïc, baby…can you more than fuck me with your insanely huge monster of a penis?"

I shake my head and let out a sound of protest. "Uh, not penis, babe. We've talked about this before."

"Fine…dick, cock, whatever. Just do it." She grabs my ass and pulls my pelvis toward her.

"Do what?" I tease, just to hear her say it again.

"Fuck me, babe…with emotion."

"I love you." I laugh as I drop my lips to hers.

FOUR

London

"I love my life."
—London Wright

The twenty-minute taxi ride from the airport goes by quickly, and before I know it, we are pulling up in front of the apartments where my sister, Georgia, lives. As I exit the cab, the hot rays of the sun beating down on my face, even this early in the day, feel marvelous. It was cold enough in Michigan this morning that I could physically see my breath.

"This is an apartment building?" Loïc asks, taking in the beautiful complex before us. "You've got to be kidding me."

"I know, right? Puts my house to shame."

"It looks like a resort." Loïc scans the stunning architecture that looks more like a five-star Cayman Islands getaway than an apartment building for college students.

"It does. You should see the incredible pools they have out back. There's some serious money here. Upper-class Cali people make rich Ann Arbor people seem poor."

"Well, I don't know about that. But college students live here?" he asks in disbelief.

I nod. "Yeah, for the most part. It's in walking distance from campus. The first time I visited Georgia here, I definitely questioned my choice to go to Michigan. Although my dad might not have sprung for such an elaborate place for me even if I had gone here anyway."

"What do you mean?"

I start walking toward the elaborate entrance. "You see, my sister…she pretends to be low maintenance. She doesn't shop as much as my mother and I do. She's more adventurous and just seems more easygoing. So, you would think that she has less than I do, right? Well, her whole go-with-the-flow attitude almost has the opposite effect. Because she doesn't ask for much, my father goes out of his way to make sure that she has the best of everything. Or it could just be because she's the baby. I don't know." I shrug as I ring the bell to my sister's apartment.

Loïc laughs. "Your dad bought you a house to live in at college, London. You're definitely not going without, little spoiled one." He kisses me on the top of my head.

"I know. I'm not complaining. I'm just saying that this apartment complex is pretty sweet, and it doesn't surprise me that my dad chose it for Georgia."

The entry door buzzes, and I open it.

Loïc grabs our bags, and we enter. "You do know that I don't make much money in the military, right?"

"Good thing I don't love you for your money then." Once we're in the foyer, I turn and wrap my arms around his backside, firmly grabbing his ass. "I love you for your tight ass." I wink.

He chuckles. "You do know that I'm going to lose that at some point, right?"

"Well, once your ass goes, all bets are off."

"Ouch," Loïc says with mock disappointment. "Well, just so you know, I will love you even when your ass sags and your face wrinkles up like a raisin."

I gasp. "That is quite possibly the most horrifying and sweetest thing anyone has ever said to me."

"I meant every word, babe."

He shoots me one of his signature smirks, and I'm tempted to ravage him right here, but sadly, it's not the time or place. So, instead, I lean up on my tiptoes and place a chaste kiss on his lips.

We take the elevator up to the top floor and walk toward the back of the building. The floor-to-ceiling windows in the hallway show a beautiful view of the pool and palm trees below. I remember that one of the biggest selling points for Georgia was this apartment's wraparound balcony with views of the pool area.

I don't bother knocking when I reach her door; instead, I walk right in.

"Londy!" My sister's high-pitched screams greet us. Her long blonde hair bounces against her shoulders as she skips toward me.

"George!" I answer in just as an annoying fashion as I throw my arms around my sister in a tight hug.

"Oh my God, it's so good to see you! I thought you would never get here!"

"It's, like, ten in the morning," I deadpan.

"I know, but you know what I mean," she responds before directing her attention toward Loïc. "You must be the new hot boyfriend. So good to meet you. You know, you're the first guy who London has allowed to meet the parents."

"That's what I hear." Loïc extends his hand to shake Georgia's.

She ignores it and hugs him instead. "I'm a hugger," she says by way of explanation.

"Loïc, my sister, Georgia. Georgia, Loïc," I introduce the two of them. "Where are Mom and Dad?" I ask.

"They should be here within the hour. They couldn't leave last night, as planned. Dad had some work stuff to do, so they left this morning."

"Is Dad really going to make it out?" I question.

"Yeah, I think he actually is. I spoke with Mom before they took off, and he was on the plane."

"Wow, I would have bet money that he would have had something work-related come up and had to cancel."

"I know. I feel like I haven't seen him in forever!" she exclaims.

"I haven't. I can't remember the last time I saw him. Oh, yeah…my graduation."

"That was the last time I saw him, too. It was only seven months ago, I guess, so not too long ago." She shrugs.

"True, but can we really count that time? He stayed for one picture after the ceremony and then had to leave. He didn't even stay for dinner."

"I know, but that's Dad." Georgia sighs. "Leave the luggage here for now. Let's go sit on the balcony. I just made a fresh batch of sangria. I tried a new recipe, and it's so good!"

"Oh, George. Drinking already?" I tease.

"Hey, it's five o'clock somewhere, right?" She's referencing the Jimmy Buffett song; he's one of my dad's favorites. He used to blast Jimmy's music all the time when we were growing up.

I grab a bottle of water from the fridge for Loïc, and we follow my sister onto the balcony. I ask about the boyfriend my sister acquired during her time gallivanting across the globe this past summer, "So, is *Fabio* going to make it out?" I murder his name with a horrible Spanish accent.

"Fabio is no more," she responds, handing me a glass of sangria before leaning back in her patio chair.

"What? What do you mean? I'm quite sure that, when you talked about him, the L word was involved," I say.

Georgia waves her hand in dismissal. "I got the L words mixed up. I might have accidentally used *love* when I meant *lust* or *loser*. Turned out that Fabio was a three-timing Latino slut. He had a girlfriend on three different continents. Prick."

"No! Why didn't you tell me?"

"Eh, I just found out this week. I figured I'd tell you in person. It's not a big deal." She shrugs.

"But you really liked him. I'm so sorry."

"I'm over it," she says nonchalantly. "He was fun for the summer, but it would have never lasted anyway."

"Well, I guess it's a good thing that I'll never meet him."

"Why's that?"

"Because I wouldn't have been able to call him by his name without laughing." I snicker.

"It is a pretty lame name." She giggles. "A lame name for a lame-ass loser. It's for the best. He had a tiny penis anyway."

I snort, almost spitting the sangria out of my mouth at the same time. "Oh my God, George," I say through laughter. "I thought things were great in that department?"

"They were decent. I mean, you know, it's not the size of the ship but the motion of the ocean anyway. But that doesn't mean I'm not going to mention it now. It was really small." She cringes.

The two of us laugh loudly, and I sneak a look toward Loïc to find him shaking his head with a grin.

Georgia addresses him, "Nothing you have to worry about. Londy tells me that everything is amazing for you both." She gives him a playful wink.

"Stop!" I protest with a smile. "You need to work on your topics-of-conversation boundaries."

"What? It's nothing that Loïc doesn't already know." She grins in her classic innocent yet mischievous way.

"That's not the point. Seriously." I chuckle. "So, anyway, your last year going well?"

"Yeah, it is." She nods.

Loïc ventures into the conversation. "So, London says you're in the environmental science program?"

"Yeah, I'm not quite sure what I'm going to do with the degree once I have it, but I'm hoping that I can do something that will have a positive impact on the environment. Maybe work for an agency or as a lobbyist."

"That's cool." Loïc nods.

"Thanks," Georgia says.

Conversation is halted by the sound of Georgia's intercom.

"Ooh, they're here! I'll go buzz them in!" she says brightly. She places her glass of sangria down on the table and heads inside.

"How are you doing?" I ask Loïc, placing my hand on his knee.

"I'm fine, babe." He smiles.

"You ready to meet the parents?"

"Sure."

"They're going to love you." I squeeze his knee.

"So you keep telling me," he replies, his lips turn up into a smirk.

"How could they not?" I lean in and place my lips against his.

Kissing Loïc calms me in a way I can't explain. His touch envelops me with something peaceful, an unwavering love. The moment his sexy mouth connects with mine, I realize that I might be a little more nervous than I thought, and I gladly pull strength from our connection.

The truth is, I want my parents to love Loïc. I need them to see how wonderful he is. I've never been one to truly crave my parents' validation, but I've never loved anyone or anything in the way I love Loïc. Of course, I don't need their approval for me to continue loving Loïc, but I have this crazy desire for them to love him simply because he deserves it.

I hesitantly pull my mouth away with a sigh. We stand, and I take Loïc's hand in mine. I lead him back into the apartment where we find Georgia and my parents embracing.

My dad releases my sister and pulls me into his arms.

"Hey, Daddy," I say, hugging him back. After hugs and kisses from my mom, I introduce Loïc. "This is my boyfriend, Loïc. Loïc, this is my mom and dad."

"Nice to meet you, Mr. and Mrs. Wright," he says as he extends his hand to shake my father's.

"Oh, call me Michael. Nice to meet you, son," my father says.

My mom pulls Loïc in for a hug. "Please call me Christine."

"Let's go sit outside, Mom. Georgia made the most delicious sangria."

"Oh, that sounds fabulous," my mom responds.

We all make our way out to the balcony.

As I walk with my mom, I hear my father talking to Loïc behind us.

"So, Christine tells me that you're in the military?"

"Yes, sir," Loïc answers.

"Army?" my dad asks.

"Currently, I'm with the Nineteenth Special Forces Group, a division of the National Guard with the Army Special Forces."

"The Green Berets?" Dad questions with a hint of awe in his voice.

"Yes, sir."

"How does that work? Did you start out in Special Forces?" Dad inquires.

"No, I was in the Army first, active duty, for six years, ever since I was eighteen. My buddy's from Michigan, and he wanted to settle down in one spot for a while, so we joined the National Guard that has a base in Ypsilanti, near his family. We're in the B Unit of the Special Forces Guard out of Ohio where we have drill one weekend a month and a two-week annual training to keep up with our specialized skills. Then, every few years, our unit is up for deployment. On deployment, we're with the airborne unit. Otherwise, we're stationed at the same base in Michigan where, for our day jobs, we're mechanics."

"Ah, I see. So, you must have had to go through some additional training for the Special Forces?"

My father sounds impressed, and I'm happy. I thought that Loïc's line of work might have been intimidating for my dad, who is more of a numbers, problem-solving, business-minded type of guy. He could never do what Loïc does, but who knows? Loïc probably wouldn't be comfortable with doing what my dad does on a daily basis either. I'm just glad that my dad sounds genuinely interested.

"Yes, sir. Quite a bit. While I was in active duty for six years, I took classes remotely and got my bachelor's degree, so I could become an officer. Then, I had a twelve-week Special Forces training. Plus, we train every month," Loïc answers.

"Well, we sure do appreciate your service, son."

"Thank you, sir."

We all sit out on the balcony.

My mom addresses Loïc, "So, tell us how you and London met."

"Mom, I already told you," I protest.

She waves me off. "I know, but I want to hear Loïc's version."

Everyone looks at Loïc.

He rubs the short stubble on his chin. "Well, I first saw her at a charity car wash thing she was doing for her sorority."

"Was it love at first sight?" Georgia asks.

"Did you notice her right away?" my mom chimes in.

"You guys!" I whine.

But my protests go ignored.

"I don't think it was love at first sight, but I definitely noticed her." Loïc pauses for a moment and lets out a small chuckle. "Though it would have been hard not to since she was making it her mission to get my attention."

I whip my head to the side to give Loïc a glare, but he pretends not to notice.

"I bet she was." Georgia nods. "I bet her boobs were practically falling out of her bikini top."

Loïc doesn't respond, but smiles shyly and exchanges a knowing look with Georgia.

"It was probably like a photo shoot straight out of a titty magazine," Georgia continues, not caring at all that this conversation is taking place in front of my parents. "London has always been able to turn anyone's attention toward her."

"Excuse me," I huff. "Um, I'm right here, and in my defense, he was wearing his military fatigues and looked darn fine. What was I supposed to do? And he didn't appear to notice me at all actually." I roll my eyes.

"I might not have shown that I noticed her, but I did. I just didn't want to give her the wrong impression because I wasn't looking for a relationship at the time," Loïc continues.

"So, what changed your mind?" my mom asks.

"Well, we kept running into each other, and I don't know…there is just something about her. She's unlike any girl I've ever known. Eventually, I couldn't fight the attraction we had, and I decided to give her a chance."

"And?" my mom asks again, like an excited teenage girl.

Loïc places his hand on my leg. "And it's going really well, better than I ever thought possible."

"Aw, that's so sweet," my mom says. "You're leaving next week?" Her tone changes to one of concern.

Loïc's eyes drop for a second before he meets my mom's expectant stare. "Yeah, I am…next Friday. I'm deploying to Afghanistan."

"That sucks," Georgia gives her two cents.

"Yeah, it's going to be hard to leave London, but it's my job."

"It's fine," I say cheerfully. "It's just a year. It will give me time to crank out a bunch of great articles and hopefully get a more prestigious journalism job. We'll be able to write letters and emails and talk on the phone pretty regularly. It will go by fast. It will be fine," I say, trying to reassure everyone, including myself.

"It will be." Loïc squeezes my leg.

"So, writing's going well?" my dad asks, switching the topic of conversation from Loïc to me.

"Really well, Dad. The online Ann Arbor news site has been featuring several of my articles every week. They seem to really like them."

"That's great, sweetie."

"Yeah, it is. I'm going to wait for a bit and keep writing for them. At some point, when I build up my portfolio enough, I want to apply to bigger papers. I want to write stories that matter, you know? I'm not going to be stuck writing about the local school district's school board president race or the university's new steps to be even more green on campus. I mean, it's okay for now, but I want to do more."

"You will. It takes time," my dad offers.

"Yeah, I know," I agree.

I'm so happy right now, sitting among the people I love more than anything in this world. If Paige were here, my level of excitement would be uncontainable. How can one person be so lucky in the joy department? For all my imperfections as a person, I must have done something right. I love my life.

We chat for a couple of hours about everything—my sister's class load, my dad's current work projects, Loïc's military history, upcoming articles I'm going to write, and my mom's adventures with acroyoga.

"I'm still not getting it, Mom," Georgia says. "So, it's like yoga but with somersaults and cartwheels and stuff?"

Mom shakes her head. "No, you're thinking gymnastics. It's yoga because it requires a lot of core strength and flexibility, but then little tricks are added in." She looks to us and obviously registers our blank faces. "Okay, so remember there is a base and a flyer. The base is usually a man but can be a strong woman. It just depends on how big the flyer is. So, I'm a flyer. That means my base—which is usually my instructor, Rob— lies on his back with his feet in the air, and then using his extended arms and legs, he pushes me up into the air. Remember when you were little, I used to hold you up with my legs in the airplane move? Well, that's one of the moves, except my arms aren't out like a plane; they're back against my sides. It's called the bird. The bird is the first basic move you learn, and I can transition to other more complicated moves from the bird position, like a pop. A pop is where Rob pushes me into the air with his hands and feet from the bird position. I tuck my legs up and land in a seated position on his feet."

"Mom, you're going to break a hip," Georgia jokes.

Mom playfully smacks her on the leg. "You'd better watch it, baby girl."

I address my dad, "So, Dad, you don't mind Mom wrestling around with this dude, Rob, every day, having his hands and feet all up in her junk?" I grin.

"It's not like that, London," Mom scolds.

Dad chuckles. "No, I don't. It's great exercise, and she loves it. Plus, I'm pretty sure Rob's gay."

Georgia huffs out a laugh. "Doesn't matter. Mom's a knockout. She could turn him straight for a day."

"Excuse me, girls, it's irrelevant whether or not Rob is gay. I would never cheat on your father, and you know that." Mom carries a hint of hurt in her voice.

"I know, Mom. We're just joking." I shoot her a grin. "What other amazing stunts do you and Rob do?"

"Uh, Christine," my dad addresses my mom before she starts to tell us about another acro move, "it's about one."

They exchange glances, and I see realization dawn in my mother's eyes.

"Oh, right!" she exclaims.

"What? Are you hungry? We can order in," Georgia offers.

"No, it's not that. There's this benefit tonight at the Canto Center for Visual Arts on campus. Your father has some colleagues he needs to chat with. You're all welcome to come. In fact, I would love it if all of you could join us. But I'm assuming you didn't bring formalwear?" she asks me.

I shake my head. "No, Mom, we didn't know anything about this benefit."

"Dad, I thought this was going to be a no-work weekend?" Georgia asks him.

My dad holds up his hands, facing his palms toward us. "It is, it is. This is a social event. I didn't know about it until yesterday. So, I'm sorry that I didn't give you more notice." He seems to notice Georgia's slight glare. "It's a good cause, Georgia, for charity." He asks my mom, "What are the proceeds going toward again, dear? Cancer research, animal shelters, rainforest preservation?"

"Um, I believe it's for ALS research. You know, Lou Gehrig's disease. Plus, I'm telling you now so that we have time to go shopping for a dress and go to a salon. It will be fun. Come with us?" she asks hopefully.

Regardless of whether or not my father's work prompted this outing is immaterial to me. I love getting all fancy for benefits.

"I'm in!" I say cheerfully. "You know I'm not going to turn down a shopping day!"

"Ugh, fine. I suppose it sounds fun," Georgia says begrudgingly.

"Looking at the shape of your nails, you're definitely due for a mani." I open my eyes wide in an exaggerated attempt at looking shocked.

"Whatever." Georgia chuckles.

"Great. Then, it's settled. Loïc, I just need your sizes, and I'll have my tux guy bring over a few options for you when he drops off my tux this afternoon."

"Um, okay," Loïc answers my dad, appearing to be slightly out of his comfort zone.

"While you ladies go dress shopping, I have some work to attend to. Is that okay with you, Georgia, love?" Dad asks with a grin.

"I suppose," Georgia huffs for effect.

"Will you be okay with fending for yourself this afternoon?" I ask Loïc. "You could hang by the pool?"

"I have the second season of *Daredevil* on my DVR, if you're interested," Georgia offers.

"Oh, really?" Loïc looks to Georgia. "I've actually been wanting to see that, but I haven't had time."

"Yeah, Fabio Fuckface wanted me to save it for him. We watched the first season on Netflix over the summer, and we were going to watch season two when he came up." She rolls her eyes.

"Language, Georgia," Mom says.

"Oh, Mom, all the classy chicks say fuck now. It's considered proper. You should try it."

Mom laughs. "I highly doubt that."

"Say it, Mom!" Georgia urges.

"No, I'm not going to."

"Say it. All the cool kids are doing it. Aren't you all trapeze yoga chill now?" Georgia quirks an eyebrow.

"It's acroyoga. And, honey, I've been around a lot longer than you, so your peer pressure has no effect on me."

"Say it! Say it! Say it! Say it!" Georgia and I chant repeatedly, clapping our hands.

My mom shakes her head in laughter.

Mom raises her hands in surrender, and we stop cheering. "All right, all right. Goodness. Fuck, girls, let's go. We have some fucking shopping to do."

I cover my mouth with my hands as I laugh loudly. Georgia looks at my mom like she has recently grown a second head.

"Um, on second thought, please don't ever say fuck in my presence again, Mom. That's just"—she shakes her head in disgust—"not okay. Not. Okay."

"Why the fuck not, George? I'm a fucking chill yoga mom."

Georgia stands abruptly. "Stop it! Just stop it! Not okay!" She plugs her ears, singing, "La-la, la-la, la-la, la-la," on her way off of the balcony.

My mom and I break out in a fit of giggles.

Finally, Mom says in almost a whisper, "Be careful what you ask for."

"Yeah, it's okay, Mom. You're plenty cool enough. No need for you to drop the F-bomb. Really."

"All right, if you say so. I just want to make my girls happy," she states in an overly joyful voice. She stands, grabs the pitcher and glasses from the table, and walks inside.

My dad stands and follows.

"You can come along while we shop, if you want. I feel bad about dragging you all the way to Cali just to leave you alone to watch TV," I say to Loïc.

"No, thanks, babe. I'm good here."

"What? You don't want to go shopping?" I ask sarcastically.

"Don't forget that I know what it's like to go shopping with you. I don't even want to imagine what it's like to go with three Wright women." He raises an eyebrow and shakes his head.

I can't help but laugh because I'm sure it would be a nightmare for any man. "I don't blame you." Closing the distance between us, I pull his mouth into a kiss. "I love you," I say, our mouths a breath apart. "Thank you for coming out here with me. I'm sure the whole meet-the-family thing isn't easy for you, but it makes me happy. So, thank you."

"Nothing about dating you is easy for me, London. It's all out of my comfort zone, but I'd face more than a few internal demons to be with you." His hand rises, tucking a lock of my hair behind my ear, before the tips of his fingers slide down the skin of my cheek, causing a torrent of goose bumps to pebble my arms.

My lips find his again as an innate desire to be joined with him takes over. Warmth invades my body as his tongue moves in time with mine, creating an intimate dance made solely for the two of us. Without breaking our connection, I leave my chair and push Loïc back into his, pressing the palms of my hands against his firm chest. I place one of my legs on either side of his thighs and straddle him.

His fingers grasp at my back, kneading my skin, as he takes the kiss deeper. An involuntary groan leaves my mouth, followed by one from Loïc. His desire surges for me, hard beneath his pants, as I grind against him. He threads his fingers through my hair, pulling me even closer to the point where I don't know where I end and he begins. We're a heated mess of tongues, lips, and skin, frantically kissing to the melody of our moans of desire. It's the sweetest song I know. Nothing is more enrapturing than the heady hum of Loïc and me on the verge of a frenzy.

A throat clears, and I pull my mouth from Loïc's as his body stiffens beneath mine.

Georgia stands behind Loïc, wearing the most amused smile. "Hey," she half-whispers, "sorry to break up this hotness"—she moves her hand in a circular motion toward Loïc and me—"but Mom's ready to leave, and I'm guessing, you really don't want her to see this."

"I'm coming," I say breathlessly.

"I'm not surprised," Georgia replies with a smirk.

"Oh my God." I bury my head against Loïc's shoulder. "Just go."

"All right, but hurry up."

"That's lovely," I say against Loïc's chest.

"Better your sister than your dad."

"Uh, definitely." I chuckle dryly. "God, I wish we were alone right now."

"Me, too. Don't worry. I'll make it all better tonight." Loïc's voice is tight and gravelly and oh-so sexy.

"Yeah, right. There's going to be zero privacy this weekend."

"Oh, we'll find some," he says reassuringly.

"I'm holding you to that."

FIVE

Loïc

"I need London—mind, body, and soul. Forever."
—*Loïc Berkeley*

I step out of the limo onto a velvety red carpet that extends from the curb and up to the walkway, ending at the large front doors of the art museum. The shiny black Gucci shoes adorning my feet feel so foreign. Hell, this entire night is straight out of the what-the-fuck-am-I-doing playbook. These shoes probably cost more than I make in a week. And this tux? I can't even think about it—or the fact that Mr. Wright insisted I keep the entire ensemble. What the hell am I supposed to do with a tux after tonight?

I don't like it, any of it—the limo, the attire, the freaking red carpet. *I mean, come on, how does all of this extravagance help people with ALS?*

Turning, I extend my arm toward the vehicle behind me. London places her soft, small hand in my grasp.

I meet her brilliant brown eyes before my gaze drops to her foot that just stepped out and the strappy black heel wrapped around it. My stare admires every inch of her as it roams up her killer leg that so perfectly stretches out between the revealing slit in her long red dress. I pull gently, helping her exit gracefully, and I pause a moment to take her in.

The lengthy dress clings to her body, accentuating all of her beautiful curves. Her hair is in loose curls that fall over the exposed skin of her back and shoulders. She's simply breathtaking, the most stunning woman I've ever seen in my life.

I take a mental picture of London for when I'm overseas, one that I can pull up anytime I need to remember her. I want to cement this vision into my mind. But, more than that, I want to be able to recall the way being here with her makes me feel—fucking fantastic, whole, and just happy.

All right, so maybe this evening isn't a total bust. I would do just about anything to be with this gorgeous woman beside me.

London loops her arm through mine. "Ready, handsome?"

It takes me a second to answer. "Yeah." I nod.

We start walking toward the entrance. London waves and smiles toward the flashing cameras.

Seriously? Who needs pictures of this? Maybe it's Stanford's college newspaper crew. For the life of me, I can't think of who else would need pictures of the people entering the benefit.

"Have I told you that you look amazing tonight?" I ask London once we get inside.

"Yes, you have—multiple times." She grins. "Have I told you that you are the hottest guy in the world and that I want to rip that tux right off of you?"

I chuckle. "No, that's a first, but I'll take it. Have I told you that I want to push you up right there next to that plaster newspaper"—I point to a sculpture on a stand beside us—"pull this sexy little number"—my finger runs lightly up her dress—"up to your waist, and fuck you against the wall, so everyone knows you're mine?"

"Ooh, no, you didn't, but I like your thinking," she answers playfully. "And I think that's a bird."

"What?" I tilt my head in question.

"The sculpture—it's a bird, not a newspaper."

I turn to the awkwardly shaped piece of plaster, squinting my eyes to study it. "That's not a bird."

"Yeah, it is." London giggles.

"Maybe a phone book or a grocery bag blowing in the wind. But a bird? I don't think so."

"Who would do a sculpture of a phone book? No one even uses phone books anymore." She laughs. "It's a bird, I swear."

"Well then, it's a freaking ugly bird."

"I'm sure the artist who made it doesn't think so," she protests. "Beauty is in the eye of the beholder, Loïc. Art is subjective."

"That might be true, but I doubt anyone here thinks this sculpture of a newspaper is pleasing to the eye."

"It's a bird!" London giggles.

"So you say." I wink. "Let's go see what other inspiring pieces we can find around here."

"Okay, but let's go to the bar first. I want a glass of wine."

"There's a bar at an art museum?"

"Of course. They put a makeshift one in here somewhere. Do you think all these people got dressed up just to look at art?"

She weaves her arm through mine once more, but this time, I follow her lead.

"You know, I've been thinking."

"Yeah?" she asks.

She stops in front of a painting that I'm quite sure is an abstract tree, but for all I know, it could be the solar system.

"I don't get this whole benefit thing. I mean, if all these people were really invested in raising money for a cause, instead of spending elaborate amounts of money on fancy clothes, limos, alcohol, you name it, wouldn't it have been a better idea to just donate that money to the cause in the first place?"

"Maybe, but that's not how it works."

"Why's that?"

"Because rich people want a party. They need a reason to donate. They need their friends to see them here and know that they donated. If you just write a check from your living room, no one will know you gave money. But everyone here knows we've donated."

"That's fucked up, London."

"Why?"

"Because, if you care about a cause, you should donate because you want to help, not because you want other people to think you're generous. I just don't get that mentality."

"I understand that. But you and I grew up with different groups of people. Right or wrong, the people I grew up with, the people my dad does work with, do care about appearances."

I narrow my eyes toward London, letting out a sigh.

"Listen, you're a better person than most people here. I know that. Don't think about the hoopla of it all. Just think of this as a party, a fun occasion where we get to dress up and have a great night out. You and I have never done anything like this together. And, not to mention, I'll donate money to any cause that puts on a party where I can see you looking all dapper and hot as hell. 'Kay?"

A smile breaks across my face. "So, you're really digging the tux, huh?"

"Heck yeah. I don't think I've ever wanted you more." She smiles widely, her full lips shining with the lip gloss that I want to kiss off.

"I love you," I reply. "Even if your love for snooty parties is a bit of a flaw."

"I'll take it. Now, let's go get me a drink!"

We find Georgia and Mrs. Wright at the bar, each with a glass of wine in hand.

"Hey! What do you think so far?" Georgia asks me.

"It's different," I answer honestly.

"He thinks we're all snobs," London chimes in.

"I didn't say that exactly." I shoot her a warning look.

Georgia huffs, "Well, we are. I mean, this tiny glass of moscato cost twenty-one dollars. What is it made out of? Golden grapes?"

"You had to pay for it?" London sounds appalled.

"Why wouldn't she have?" I ask, confused.

"Normally, the alcohol is free at these events. I mean, our tickets to get in cost a lot. We shouldn't have to pay for alcohol, too."

"Right, because any extra money should go toward booze instead of the charity," I say dryly.

London playfully smacks my arm.

"There is a free wine list, but you know those are the five-dollar-a-bottle wines from the local supermarket.

Plus, Daddy opened a tab and told us to purchase our drinks with it," Georgia says.

"Oh, good. Do you want anything, Loïc?" London asks.

"I'm good with water, thanks."

London gives our drink order to the bartender.

"Oh, look. It's the Petersons!" Mrs. Wright says excitedly.

She'd been so quiet that I almost forgot she was standing here.

"No, Mom," Georgia says firmly.

"Come on, honey. Patrick has his MD now. He's a surgeon."

"I don't care. He's, like, ten years older than me, and he is so annoying."

"Oh, that's not fair," Mrs. Wright argues, looking so much like London. "It's been years since you've seen him, and I think he's only, like, seven years older."

"Exactly, Mom. I haven't seen him since we lived in Sacramento. I doubt they even remember us."

"Oh, no, they do. I'm Facebook friends with Carol, and we see each other from time to time at these kinds of events. Just come say hi," Mrs. Wright pleads, taking Georgia's hand.

"I bet you wish Fabio were here now, don't ya?" London giggles.

"Ew, no. But, if I had known Mom was going to go all matchmaker on me, I would have invited Ben."

"Who's Ben?" London asks.

"Just a guy I've been hooking up with," Georgia answers casually.

"But you just broke up with Fabio?" London questions, her voice rising an octave.

Georgia scoffs, "Yeah, like, almost a week ago."

"Oh my goodness! Where did I go wrong with you two?" Mrs. Wright shakes her head.

"Hey! Don't lump me in with Georgia. I'm in a relationship," London protests.

Mrs. Wright lets out a sigh. "Let's go, Georgia. You could stand a conversation with some people with class."

"Hey, I'm offended. How do you know my booty call, Ben, doesn't have class, Mom? And he's religious, too. He's always calling out to God when he's in my bed. It's very sweet," Georgia says seriously.

London bends over in laughter.

I can't stop the smile that spreads across my face. This entire exchange is comical. I don't know how I expected London's family dynamic to be, but it wasn't like this.

"Come on, Georgia," Mrs. Wright says wearily.

"Just go," London urges with a giggle. "You're causing Mom to age, like, ten years right in front of us."

"Fine, but I'm talking to *Patrick Peterson*," she says his name in a nasally voice, "for only five minutes, and if his fingers go anywhere near his nose, I'm throwing this glass of wine at him."

"I'm sure he wasn't picking his nose, honey. He was probably itching it. And he was fifteen. Cut him some slack," Mrs. Wright says.

"Exactly. He was fifteen. I was eight, and I knew that picking your nose in front of someone was disgusting! And then he just continued eating his hamburger without washing his hands first!"

Georgia and Mrs. Wright continue to argue about the apparent nose-picking incident as they walk away.

"Wow," I say to London.

"I know."

"Your family is awesome, especially Georgia."

"Yeah, she's a feisty one. Everyone adores her. She has next to zero filter and can be so crude, but everyone loves her. There's just something endearing about her."

"Maybe because she's so different than everyone here. She's like a breath of fresh air."

"Hey, just because people have money doesn't mean that they all walk around with sticks up their butts. There are some cool people here."

"Really? Besides your family, who?"

"Uh, Patrick Peterson. He's a surgeon. Duh," she says in a valley girl voice.

I let out a chuckle. "Yeah, well, he picks his nose, which cancels out the cool doctor thing he has going on."

She shrugs. "True. So, let's go look at more art, shall we?" She hands me a water before taking a sip of her wine. "Mmm, this is good. It must be made out of golden grapes."

London entwines her free hand through mine as we weave through the crowd of elaborately dressed people to look at the different art pieces.

One thing's for sure; London and I do not have the same taste in art or even the same perspective. Sure, we both recognize the painting of a chair to be just that—a painting of a chair—yet London thinks it represents loneliness, whereas I think it represents dinnertime.

"Okay, what about this one?" London asks.

We stand in front of an abstract painting with lots of splattered colors, some wavy lines, and tons of paint dribbles.

When I don't answer, she continues, "I think the artist is trying to represent a state of joy in a life filled with chaos. There's something happy and sorrowful about it at the same time, you know?"

I tilt my head to the side and really look at the painting. "I think the artist is a four-year-old from the local preschool."

London laughs. "Stop! Really, try to see something."

"I can't. They're just colors thrown onto a canvas, London. There's no rhyme or reason to it."

"Right, so maybe it represents life in that way?"

"Maybe," I answer hesitantly.

"You know, there's no wrong answer, babe."

"Really? That's not what you said about the newspaper sculpture." I peer down to her.

She rolls her eyes. "Because that was clearly a bird!"

"Nope, newspaper," I say shortly.

She shakes her head. "I hate you," she says with a smile.

"And I love you, babe." I lean in and kiss her forehead. "Okay, let me try again." I stand up straight and face the painting.

"Oh, good." London says and faces the painting, too.

"I spy with my little eye…a woman in a tight red dress."

"No, you don't." London giggles.

"Oh, yeah…yeah, I do. Right here." I point toward the glob of red paint in the middle of the canvas. "And, oh…do you see this black squiggly line? That is me as I approach the woman, who's drop-dead gorgeous, by the way. Her eyes are big and a beautiful brown with flecks of gold. And her lips…" I allow my head fall back as I let out a sigh.

"Tell me about her lips," London urges.

I look at the painting again. "Well, they're perfect…plump and full…and so kissable." I circle my hand above the top right portion of the canvas, which holds a bunch of paint swirls. "This, right here, is the man

53

taking the woman. She's so gorgeous that he had to have her immediately…so they strolled off to the corner of the room. He's holding her against a wall and pounding into her as she screams his name."

"Oh, wow. That escalated quickly."

I nod. "Yep…sure did."

"What about all of this right here?" London points to the squiggles surrounding the swirly paint in the corner.

"Well, those are all of the other people watching, of course. How could they not? When this couple gets together, it's pretty astounding."

London turns to me and grabs my arm. "We should go find a corner."

"What?" I question.

"I want it. I want your version of the painting…just minus the watching crowd." She grins.

"London…" I turn and face her, and I place my finger beneath her chin. Tilting her face up toward mine, I press my lips against hers, taking her in a soft kiss. I pull away. "We can't."

"Uh, yeah, we can. What's up? We've done it in public places before. Remember the Mexican restaurant restroom?"

"Yeah, but your dad wasn't in the Mexican restaurant with us. He would be mortified and embarrassed if we got caught. Not to mention, he'd hate me forever."

"Then, we won't get caught. Come on," she says with a mischievous smile.

Damn it if I'm not instantly hard.

"All right, but we have to find someplace good."

"Look at you, being all responsible." She laughs as she takes my hand.

I chuckle. "This hardly counts as being responsible, London."

"Yeah, whatever." She waves her free hand through the air in a motion of nonchalance.

We quickly head down the hallway toward the back of a large room that hosts some of the art pieces. Sneaking down the empty hallway, we pass what seem to be offices. London checks each door, but they're all locked.

We turn another corner, and at the end of a narrow hall is an exit door. As we get closer, we notice a door beside the exit. London twists the handle, and it opens. It appears to be a janitor's closet. Against the far wall are cleaning supplies, a mop, and a bucket. Along the left side is a workbench that—save for a couple of tools, which we hurriedly push to the side—is clean.

"Best part? The door locks," London says with a huge grin as she turns the deadbolt.

The moment she turns back around, I crash my mouth against hers. Threading my hands through her curly locks, I pull her closer. She opens her mouth on a groan, and my tongue hastily enters. We kiss with reckless abandon. Tongues tasting. Hands feeling. Mouths moaning. Bodies shaking with desire.

My entire body vibrates with intense need.

That's the entirety of it right there. I need London— mind, body, and soul. Forever.

I love everything about her, even the things I shouldn't. I find her spoiled nature—though she's become less so as we've gotten to know each other—cute somehow. I love her witty personality and the way she always keeps me on my toes. Instead of pissing me off, like it should, the way she always challenges me turns me on like no one else ever has. I've become addicted to the way in which she loves me. Her love invades my body every day, filling me with a happiness that I've never known.

And this, right here, the way our bodies come together as if they were always meant to, as if they were the two opposing halves in a two-piece puzzle, I've never experienced anything close to the way I feel when I'm with London.

God, I love her.

"I need you, baby," I say gruffly between panting, raw breaths, my palms now grasping her hips.

"You have me," she says breathlessly against the skin of my neck.

As she licks from the collar of my shirt to my jaw, I grab ahold of the zipper at her side and slowly pull down. She shimmies the dress off until it falls at her feet. She stands before me in a strapless bra and a thong, looking like she stepped straight out of my dreams. I unclasp her bra and let it fall to the ground. My pulse leaps when she pushes down her red lacy thong.

I clear my throat. "Hell yes, this is exactly how I want you." My eyes scan her perfect naked body.

She gives me a sexy smirk as she unzips my dress pants. Pushing my boxers and pants down to my thighs, she fists my dick. "And this is how I want you—in your tux, the only bare part being the one that's going to be inside me."

I thread my fingers through London's hair once more, my mouth moving in a frenzy across her neck. I kiss down her body, paying attention to all her soft and sensitive parts. She moans as her back falls against the closet door behind her. Falling to my knees, I grab one of her ankles, right above where the strap of her high heel buckles. Lifting her leg, I bring it up until it's draped over my shoulder, allowing me precise access to what I want to taste the most. My tongue moves languidly against her opening. She groans, grasping at my hair with one hand, while she digs her fingers into my shoulder with her other hand to steady herself.

"Loïc…" Her voice sounds almost pained as my name comes from her lips.

"I got you." My tongue continues its assault alternating with my lips that suck gently. Using two fingers, I enter her and rub against her front wall.

London's body starts to quiver. She lets her head fall back against the door as breathy moans fill the small space. She begins wildly bucking her hips while forcefully pulling my hair.

"Oh God, Loïc, yes. *Loïc…*" The second time she says my name, it's more of a cry as her entire body starts to shake.

I continue to lick softly as her trembles slow. When she's finished, I take her leg from my shoulder and place her foot back on the ground. I kiss up her body until I'm facing her. Her eyes aren't completely focused as she lets out long breaths.

"Good?" I inquire smugly.

"The best," she sighs out.

I grab the bottom of her ass cheeks and pull her up. She wraps her legs around my back. My lips find hers as I guide myself into her entrance. We moan collectively as I fill her completely. Digging my fingers into her ass, I start moving. She's warm and wet and so fucking amazing.

I ravage her mouth, my tongue almost mimicking the movements below. I pound into her with a hot, fiery abandon, as if I can't get enough. And I can't. It's never hard enough, deep enough, fast enough, or long enough. I always want more with London. Our connection is damn near perfection, and I want more. With her, I'll always need more.

I bury my face against her neck. I can taste the salt on her damp skin and feel the soft vibrations of her moans against my lips. Her body starts to quake, and I feverishly pound into her. With each thrust, the small space fills with the rhythmic sounds of the door moving against the metal hinges and our cries of pleasure as we desperately chase our release. London finds hers first, and I follow right behind her, groaning low and deep, as my body empties within her warmth.

I hold London against me as we work to calm our breaths.

After a few minutes, she says, "My love of snooty parties isn't that much of a flaw now, is it?"

"Hell no, especially if they all include fucking like that in a closet."

"Will you be wearing a tux to all future benefits that we attend?" she asks.

"Um, yeah?" I answer hesitantly, not sure of where she's going with this.

"Then, there will definitely be closet-fucking at future benefits." She smiles.

"Yep…then definitely not a flaw. I actually love these types of things."

London laughs. "I knew I could turn you."

"Well, we didn't do a very good job of being quiet. I think it's safe to say that anyone passing through this hallway could have heard us."

"It's hard to be quiet when it's so good," she responds. "And don't worry; no one's walking around here. They're all enjoying the art and the party."

"Let's hope so," I answer as I look around.

Spotting a roll of paper towels, I hold London up with one hand and use my other one to rip off a long sheet. I hand it to London before setting her down.

We both wipe up as best we can before discarding the dirty paper towels in the trash can next to the mop.

"God, I'm fucking hot as hell," I say.

"Yes, you are," London says in a seductive voice.

I lower my stare. "I mean, technically. I'm pretty sure my entire undershirt is drenched with sweat. It's a sauna in here."

"Yeah, I don't think there are any AC vents in here. It's like a weird steam room that smells of sex, sweat, and bleach."

London pats her skin dry, so she can pull up the tight dress. I fix my attire and pat down my hair.

"How do I look?" London asks, holding her arms out to the sides and spinning.

"Sexy."

"But not the I've-just-been-fucked sexy, right?"

I bite my lip. "I don't know, babe. I think your curls are a little messier than before?"

She waves a hand in dismissal. "It's fine. No one will notice."

We exit the closet to an empty hallway, and it's immediately twenty degrees cooler out here.

Thank God.

We follow the set of halls until we're back in the main room.

"Thirsty?" London asks.

"Definitely," I answer.

We head toward the bar, and we're almost there when Georgia intercepts us.

"There you are. I've been looking—" She stops mid thought. "Wait a minute." Her eyes scan between London and me. "You two just flipping did it somewhere, didn't you?"

"Um, I have no idea what you're talking about." London shrugs. "How was Booger Boy?"

"Well, he had the decency not to go digging for gold tonight." She holds her hands up. "Wait, you're not changing the subject. You two just did it. Admit it."

"So?" London shrugs again, but this time, she carries a guilty grin.

"OMG…I'm normally the scandalous one. What are you doing to my sister, Loïc?"

Before I can answer, London says, "Satisfying me."

I turn to London, surprised, and then look to see Georgia's reaction.

She's nodding her head. "Hmm," she says. "Well, can't argue with that. But, Londy, babe…your hair definitely looks like you washed it with a full bottle of Just Been Fucked shampoo."

"Really?" London asks.

"Yeah, and your chest is a little red." Georgia nods toward London's chest, which is, in fact, a little splotchy.

"Well, the chest thing is fine. I get red when I drink too much wine, and I've been drinking a lot tonight." She winks at her sister. "Can you find me a ponytail holder? I'll just put my hair up. You know, I guarantee Mom has one in her purse."

"I'm on it. I'll meet you at the bar." Georgia takes off.

When Georgia meets us at the bar, she hands London a hair tie before saying, "I get that you two can't keep your hands off each other, but that was a bold move, doing it here."

"Well, we knew we wouldn't get a chance any other time this weekend. So, we thought, why not?" London answers as she swoops her hair up into a ponytail.

"Why's that?" Georgia asks.

"Why's what?" London responds.

"Why won't you get another chance this weekend?"

"Because, obviously, with us all staying at your place, it doesn't leave much privacy," London says.

"Mom and Dad are staying at a hotel. You and Loïc get the guest bedroom, silly." Georgia chuckles.

"Really? Why didn't I know that?" London almost shrieks with giddiness.

"I have no idea. You're not very observant though. That's always been the plan. Didn't you wonder why Mom and Dad didn't have any luggage with them? They checked into the hotel before they came over this morning." Georgia shakes her head and grins. "You two are a little lost in your La-La Loveland."

"Huh. Well, sweet!" London responds.

"This weekend just got a hell of a lot better," I cut in, to which the three of us start laughing.

SIX

London

"I thought my life was perfect before Loïc, but the longer I'm with him, the more I realize that it was lacking in so many ways."
—London Wright

I know that I've recently professed Michigan to be my home, but sitting out on a balcony overlooking palm trees and a pool while sipping coffee in almost seventy degree weather at eight o'clock in the morning in November sounds more like a proper home, a home that I would love.

"I love it here," I sigh dreamily. "Why on earth did I choose to go to college in Michigan?"

"I don't remember. Was it because the University of Michigan is an amazing school?" Georgia says.

"Eh, I'm not sure. Yes, it is. But wasn't there another reason?"

"A boy?" Georgia asks.

"Heck no. I didn't choose my college based off of a crush." I think of how I'm now planning my life around Loïc, but that's different somehow. What I have with Loïc is real love, and that trumps everything else.

"We never lived there, did we?" Georgia scrunches up her face in concentration.

I can't help but laugh. "Isn't it crazy that we have to seriously think about where we've lived?"

"I know! Come to think of it, I think we were living in Chicago when you applied to school at U of M."

"You're right! I added Michigan to my list of college tours because of that lawyer friend of Dad's who told me it was the best school ever."

"Penis!" Georgia giggles.

I follow suit. "Yes, Mr. Penis!" I believe his correct surname was Penash, but Georgia and I'd use our preferred last name for him—behind his back, of course.

"Whatever happened to Mr. Penis?"

"Who knows? I haven't seen him since Chicago." I shrug.

"That's so strange because he and his wife used to come to our house all the time for dinner parties."

"I know, but that's how it is with Dad's friends. They're always changing based on his location."

"Well, cheers to Mr. Penis for getting you interested in Michigan. You would never have met Loïc or Paige had you not gone there."

Georgia holds up her coffee cup, and I gently tap mine against hers in an odd morning toast.

"True. I think I chose Michigan because I had the most fun tour there. Yes, their academics are great, but their parties are pretty amazing."

"It was nice seeing Mom and Dad, huh?" Georgia asks, changing the subject.

"It was. I was glad that Dad stayed all day yesterday. I can't remember the last time we've spent two entire days with him."

"It was great," Georgia agrees. "Any thoughts on what you want to do when Loïc comes back?"

Loïc's currently out, running. Today's our last day in California, and a few minutes ago, Georgia listed off some possible activities we could do. I've been thinking about our options while we've been out here, sipping coffee.

"Yeah, I think Santa Cruz sounds fun."

"Sweet! Santa Cruz, it is! I love it there," Georgia says with excitement.

An hour and a half later, Georgia is parking in a space along Pacific Avenue, which is a picturesque tree-lined street with adorable little shops and cafés. We grab our beach bags and start walking toward the water.

"If you get bored of the beach, we can always head to the Beach Boardwalk," Georgia suggests. "It's like an old-fashioned amusement park. It's fun."

"That does sound fun," I agree. "I definitely want to show Loïc what a real beach day is like. He likes to do all these exhausting activities when he takes me to the beach. Right, babe?" I playfully nudge Loïc in the side.

"To which activity are you referring? The boogie-boarding or the other activity we did in the water? Because, if I remember correctly, you didn't complain about that." He shoots me a wink.

I shake my head and laugh. "I was talking about the boogie boards, of course."

"Well, that doesn't really pertain here. You're not going to want to get in the water anyway. It's freezing this time of year," Georgia informs us.

"There are a few surfers out in the water," I mention, looking out to the water as one of them rides a wave to shore.

"Yeah, but they have serious wet suits on. Most people aren't swimming in the water right now."

"I don't know. Lake Michigan is pretty damn cold early summer, and I manage," Loïc offers.

"You go for it, babe," I scoff. "I think I'll hang on the beach."

"If I go in, you're going in with me."

"Don't you dare." I scowl at him. "I hate being cold."

"It's an adventure," he teases me.

"That's right—one you can go on yourself." I narrow my eyes toward him in warning.

Georgia lays down the beach blanket on the sand. "I agree with London on this one. It might be okay to walk along the beach and dip your toes, but I wouldn't want to go in. No way."

"All right. I'm going to run across the street to one of the stores. I'll be back," Loïc says to us.

"You go for it, babe. We'll be here, relaxing and enjoying our beach day." I smile lazily and lie back on the blanket.

"You two have great chemistry," Georgia says to me after Loïc's left.

"You think?"

"Yeah, totally. I can see why you're so enamored with him."

"I really love him, George. I feel in my heart that he's the one, you know?"

"I see that, and you're probably right. I can picture you marrying him."

"I'm going to—someday. I just know it, but I'm in no rush. So, what's up with this Ben guy?"

Georgia laughs beside me. "Oh, we're just friends with benefits, nothing more."

My sister and I chat and soak in the incredible California sun.

I've missed her. It's hard being on the other side of the country from her, but I guess that's what happens when people grow up. I'm so grateful I've had this long weekend with her, especially since she's been able to meet and hang out with Loïc before he heads overseas.

All at once, I'm shrouded in shadow, and I open my eyes to find Loïc standing beside me with a gigantic grin and two large surfboards.

"Hell no," I argue before he has a chance to say a word.

He tosses a wet suit onto my lap. "Suit up, baby."

"Loïc," I whine more than is probably acceptable for someone my age. But I don't care. That water is cold, and the thought of going in it does not make me happy. "Are you serious?"

"Yep, we're doing this. Come on, it will be fun."

"Are you incapable of just relaxing?" I huff out.

"Babe, we can't come to Cali and not take advantage of the waves."

"Um, I beg to differ. Plus, I can't surf."

"I'll teach you."

"You can surf?" I tilt my head to the side.

"Of course."

"Jeez, is there anything you can't do?" I chuckle.

Loïc doesn't answer, but seriously, the guy is like an outdoor-sports-enthusiast master. I stand reluctantly and grab the wet suit.

"Before you put that on, let's practice on the beach." Loïc starts to walk away.

I shoot my sister a save-me glare, to which she only laughs, and I hesitantly follow Loïc.

Loïc lays our boards flat on the sand. "Before we take it to the water, you need to practice getting up on your board. You can get the technique down perfectly on land so that it won't be as difficult when you're out in the water."

"Okay."

Loïc proceeds to show me the steps to getting up on the board, and I practice—a lot.

Standing on the board with my hands out to the sides, I pretend I'm on the water. "I totally got this!" I giggle, proud of myself.

"Let's get our suits on, and we'll go out," he suggests.

"Great!"

Loïc's love of surfing has officially rubbed off on me, like everything that he introduces me to does. I'm actually excited to get out there in the cold ocean and try to get up on an actual wave.

We suit up. Lying on our stomachs, we paddle out into the water. It's a little chilly, but honestly, with the suit on, it's not that bad. Once we're out far enough, we paddle the boards around so that we're facing the beach, and we wait for a wave. We're not too far out from land. Loïc is starting me on little waves, which is definitely for the best.

"Paddle!" Loïc commands.

I listen as I swipe my arms through the water on the sides of my board.

"Up, London!" he yells.

I try to do exactly like I did on land.

The truth is, it is a hell of a lot harder to get up onto your board when you're balancing on the water. I fall to the side, splashing into the ocean. Beneath the water, I swim upward until my head breaks the water's surface, and I take a breath. Looking around, I see Loïc riding the wave toward the shore. Using more arms strength than I thought I had, I pull myself out of the water and onto the board. I wait while Loïc paddles back out toward me.

"I suck," I say, defeated.

He laughs. "You don't. Of course you weren't going to get up on your first try. You'll get there. Come on, let's paddle back out and try it again."

We repeat this process nine times, the outcome always the same as the first time. I'm exhausted. My entire body is screaming in pain as muscles I've never used weep for mercy. My arms shake from exertion, and my lungs burn. My cheeks are drenched with salt water— from the ocean or my own tears, I'm not sure. But I'm done. I'm definitely not a surfer.

I lay my head on my board, unable to pull my weak body atop it, and wait for Loïc to swim out to me.

"You okay?" he questions when he reaches me.

"I can't do it again," I whimper weakly.

"Baby, you can do it. I know you can." Loïc's voice is lined with amusement, but I'm too tired to care.

I'm sure I look like a sniffling wimp, and I'm cool with that as long as I can be finished with this surfing adventure.

"Can I go in?" I plead.

"Look at me, London."

I lift my head from the board and stare into his beautiful blues. "You can do this. I know it. Let's try it one more time, and promise me that you'll give it everything you've got."

"Okay." I nod.

So, we repeat the process again, swimming out a little ways before turning our boards toward land.

Loïc tells me when to start paddling as the wave starts to build. Then, he yells, "Now!"

I grab ahold of the sides of the board and hoist my body up into a standing position. My feet land exactly where they should, and I stand with my arms out to my sides.

Oh my God, I'm doing it!

I manage to stay atop my board as the wave carries me toward shore. With my arms outstretched and the ocean breeze in my face, I feel like I'm flying. It's the most incredible, freeing feeling in the world.

The board hits the beach, and I bend to remove the Velcro strap attached to my ankle.

I sprint toward Loïc and throw myself into his arms, wrapping my legs around his waist. "I did it! I did it! It was so amazing," I screech as I cling to him.

His strong body shakes with laughter beneath mine, and he hugs me tight. "Awesome, right?"

"So awesome. I loved it."

"I knew you would."

We head back out into the water, and I'm able to ride two more waves in. Though I desperately want to, I can't manage another. I've never been so sore in my entire life.

Once again, Loïc urged me to do something that I would never have done without him, and I ended up loving it. I thought my life was perfect before Loïc, but the longer I'm with him, the more I realize that it was lacking in so many ways. He brings a zest for life that I didn't have on my own. He helps me push my limits, and because of that, I'm a better person, a more fulfilled one. I was cruising through life on autopilot, but with Loïc, I'm actually living it, and it's awesome.

"Oh my God, you have to try that, George. It's so fun," I say as I fall on the blanket. "You can use my wet suit. Loïc will teach you."

"I know. I love surfing," she replies.

"I didn't know you surfed."

"Of course. I live in California, Londy," she says by way of explanation. "I'm good though. We should pack up and go get something to eat before heading back. I don't want you to be running late for your flight."

"Stupid flight," I grumble.

Loïc and I are taking the red-eye back to Michigan tonight. I wish we didn't have to. It would be great to hide away from life in California with the ocean and warm sun. Back in Michigan, we're going to be stepping off the plane into coldness—in more ways than one. Not only is the weather freezing, but the looming date of Loïc's departure also gives me a chill. I can't even think about it.

I just want to flee reality and get lost here in paradise, but unfortunately, that's not an option.

SEVEN

Loïc

Age Fifteen

Amarillo, Texas

"Because of everything I've lost, I can't lose Sarah, too."
—Loïc Berkeley

I wake with a start. My back pushes into the gravel beneath it before I jolt up. I reach my arm out to the side, patting the spot beside me, and I immediately notice that Sarah isn't there. Her comforting warmth is unmistakably missing.

Something's wrong.

I'm surrounded by darkness, save for the tiny tease of light rising from the horizon in the distance, indicating dawn's impending arrival. It's early.

Sarah would never just leave me. She wouldn't.

"Sarah! Sarah!" I call out.

A sad echo of my voice bounces back from the metal above me.

We've been staying under this overpass for about a week now. I found some temporary work in town that pays me cash to sort and load produce onto trucks. It's long hours and tiring work, but I can't turn down money. Plus, I'd rather be working than standing on a street corner, holding up a cardboard sign, begging for handouts, even though the latter scenario has been more familiar as of late. Not too many people are willing to hire a teenage boy with no identification and a less than desirable appearance. I'm hoping my current employer will keep me around long enough, so I can afford to get a few clean sets of clothes and some newer shoes for Sarah and me from the Salvation Army, and we could each use a haircut. I'm sure I could get more work if I looked better.

Sarah and I try to stay clean. Every day, we brush our teeth and wash up at gas station restrooms, and at least twice a week, we pay to take showers at truck stops.

Maybe she had to go to the bathroom? I walk to the edge of the overpass. The loud traffic sounds overhead, and the metal shakes as large trucks zoom across.

"Sarah!" I call out.

Nothing.

I pace around, continuing to call her name. There's no response.

Where could she be?

Sarah and I are very careful. We don't split up often, and when we do, we make specific plans as to when and where we will meet up. It's not like I can just call her. She's never just left without telling me before.

A vague memory from when I was young surfaces. My dad and I were standing in front of an amusement park of some sort, and he was going over what I should do if I got separated from him. I remember him telling me to stay put, that if I stayed right where I was, then he could backtrack to all the places we'd been until he found me.

Stay put.

Should I just wait here and hope she returns? This thought doesn't sit well with me. *What if she's hurt? In trouble? Lost?*

I can't imagine the latter. Sarah's better with directions than I am. She'd be able to find her way back here.

Unless…

All the ways in which Sarah could need me enter my mind. *What if she was found? What if she's been picked up by social services? What if she's screaming for me to help her?*

I have to find her. But where do I start?

With my arms raised to my head, my fingers grasp my hair, pulling.

Where do I look? Where do I look? I think as I bend at the waist, the feeling of dread pulling me down.

Suddenly, I think about the corner where she panhandled a couple of times this week while I was working. I remember her telling me about a guy who works at the grocery store right there.

Pedro is his name.

Yes, Pedro, and he brought her a delicious deli sandwich from the store for lunch the past two days. She spoke about him like she had developed a friendship of sorts with him.

Maybe he's seen her today? Or perhaps she mentioned something to him yesterday when she was there?

It's somewhere to start at least.

I stash my backpack and our bedding between where the beam from the bridge meets the ground. A large section of metal is bent up away from the earth at a ninety-degree angle, creating an ideal hiding place for our belongings. It's come in handy this week, allowing us to leave our heavy satchels behind while we worked.

It only takes a moment to put our things away, and then I'm off, walking toward town. With each step, I pray that I find Sarah. I'm hoping this is all an oversight on my end. Perhaps, she mentioned to me that she had work early this morning, and I simply don't remember her telling me.

Maybe I was half-asleep when she mentioned it? It has to be something like that. Nothing else makes sense.

I replay our conversations in my mind as I walk, desperately trying to remember anything that I missed. I reach the small grocery store and almost walk into the sliding glass doors when they don't automatically open.

Crap. The store hasn't opened yet.

My jaw clenches, and my posture is stiff and rigid as I pace in front of the closed doors. I start walking and scan the area. It's not much, but it's something until I can talk to Pedro. I make my way around the store until I find myself in a side alley full of rusted blue dumpsters. I turn to head back in the other direction when I see it.

A foot.

It's bare, lying against the paved ground, as it peeks out from the other side of the waste receptacle.

I run to it, and when I come around the large metal container full of trash, I gasp. It's Sarah. Her eyes are closed, and she's naked from the waist down.

"Sarah!" I call out as I fall to my knees and shake her shoulders. "Sarah!" My voice is heavy with emotion, and my vision blurs.

She grunts, and I let out a sigh of relief, a small one at least. *Why in the hell is she lying here, half-naked and unconscious?* I continue to gently move her shoulders back and forth as I say her name over and over.

Eventually, she stirs and opens her eyes. She blinks heavy, once…twice, and then she stares. Her eyes widen with fear. "Loïc?" she asks, her voice broken and gravelly.

"I'm here, Sarah." I pull her chest up to mine and hug her against me. "What happened? Are you okay? Why did you leave? Where are your clothes?" The questions come out in rapid succession. I shake my head, expelling a large breath, before asking again, "Are you okay?"

She nods against my chest as I hold her to me.

"Where are your pants?" I ask softly.

She pulls back and looks down at her exposed skin. "Um…" She looks around. "I'm not sure. They should be…" She leans to the side to look around me. "They should be close?" Her statement sounds more like a question. "I don't know."

"Here." I stand, pulling her up with me. I take off my T-shirt and hold the neck hole open wide. Bending on one knee, I position the shirt in front of her feet. "Step in."

She does as I said, and I shimmy the T-shirt up her legs. I have to rip the fabric a little to get it up over her hips, but the shirt is old and worn and actually stretches fairly easily.

I look down at her makeshift skirt and shrug. "Well, it will have to do until we get back. Let's get out of here." I take note of her bare feet. "Do you want me to carry you?"

She shakes her head. "No, I'll be careful. I'll watch where I'm stepping."

I nod. "All right, let's go."

I lead us back toward our spot beneath the bridge as quickly as I can without risking Sarah hurting herself.

Once we're there and she's dressed in some of her own clothes, we sit next to each other against the coarse grassy hill on the side of the bridge.

"What happened? Why did you leave?"

"I'm sorry. I meant to get back before you woke up." Her voice is quiet.

"Please just tell me what is going on," I plead softly.

She pulls her knees up to her chest and wraps her arms around them. "Well, I went to meet Pedro last night. I left after you fell asleep because I didn't want you to worry about me."

"Did he ra-rape you?" I struggle to get the word out.

"No. I offered, I think."

"You don't remember?"

She sighs. "Not much, no. I took some stuff. I was kind of out of it."

My heart pounds fiercely in my chest as I register her words. "What kind of stuff? Like drugs?"

She nods.

"You met him for drugs?" I ask, my voice quivering in disbelief.

She nods again.

"Why?"

"He offered, and I wanted it…to escape, you know? Just for a bit. I won't do it again. I just needed a break from it all for one night." Her voice is so hollow, and it causes my heart to shatter.

I wish I could kill every man who has ever hurt her.

"I'm here for you, Sarah. You can talk to me about anything. I'll help you, and if I can't, I'll figure out how. You're not alone."

She leans her face against her knees. The palm of my hand splays across her back as she shakes violently with her sobs. I don't know what else to say, so I remain silent as she cries, and I continue to rub her back.

After a while, her sobs abate, and she rocks to the side, allowing her body to fall into mine. I wrap my arms around her back and hold her tight.

"We'll get through this. You know that, right? It's going to get better. I'll help you. I'll do anything to make things better for you, Sarah, but I can't help you if I lose you. You can't leave me like that again. What if I hadn't been the one to find you? What if the cops had found you, and they sent you back? We have to be careful."

"I know." She sniffles. "It was stupid. I won't do it again."

"Okay," I sigh. "Good. Do you need anything?"

"Just this. Just you. Please hold me for a bit. Don't let me go just yet," she whispers.

"Sarah, I'll never let you go. As long as I'm alive, I'm going to protect you. I'll keep you safe. I'll make everything better. You just have to trust me." Even as I say the words, I know they're empty promises. They sound immature and naive as they come from my mouth. But that doesn't change the fact that I want to believe them.

The reality is that, in this world, one can want to do something with the greatest desire, but the fact is that one has very little control over the actual trajectory of their path. I know because I've wanted many things in my life, and I've lost them all.

Regardless, I want my words to be true this time. Because of everything I've lost, I can't lose Sarah, too.

And, as much as I want my promises to be true for Sarah's sake, I want them to be true for mine as well. I've tried so hard to be brave my entire life, and I do have the courage to fight for us, for our happiness. But I know that I'll lose it all if I fall short. If I fail Sarah, I won't have the courage to fight anymore.

EIGHT

London

*"True love is forever, but so is true friendship,
and I can't live without either."*
—London Wright

I light the last candle atop the triple-layered cake that I picked up from an incredible little bakery down the street. The soft glow of the flames dance across the icing, illuminating the edible sugar flowers that adorn the cake. It's almost too pretty to eat, but with the chocolate mouse filling inside, I know it's going to taste even more spectacular than it looks.

Placing my hands beneath the dish that holds the cake, I slowly walk it out to the living room where the birthday girl sits, surrounded by a group of our girlfriends. The room fills with the traditional "Happy Birthday" song as we serenade Paige.

"Make a wish," I say when the song is finished.

Paige closes her eyes as she blows out the candles, and we all clap.

"Love you, Paige." I smile down to my best friend.

"Love you, too." She grins up at me.

As I take the cake back into the kitchen to slice it up, our sorority sister Kristyn comes out of the kitchen with a cooler of her famous Jell-O shots, yelling, "It's party o'clock!" to which the group of girls in the living room cheer.

Paige and I don't hang out with our old sorority sisters very often, but every time we do, it's so much fun.

I put pieces of cake onto plates and smile to myself as the music from the living room and the laughter of our friends gets louder. There's nothing like an all-girl celebration. The presence of guys makes girls stupid. It's a sad fact. It never fails. If guys were here, at least one of our friends would end up crying. The list of possible emotions causing the tears is endless—jealousy, anger, hurt. The list goes on. A no-boys-allowed party is so much better.

Yet I miss Loïc so much. He leaves in less than a week, and I'm starting to panic. I don't know what I'm going to do without him.

Stop it, London!

I swore to myself that I wouldn't allow my thoughts to be overcome by Loïc tonight. Today is Paige's day. Yes, I love Loïc, so missing him is real. But I love Paige, too. True love is forever, but so is true friendship, and I can't live without either.

We dance, drink, eat, take pictures, and laugh. It's perfect.

Shortly after eleven, I get a call.

"The limo's here!" I yell out when I get off the phone.

We ask the driver to take pictures of our group in front of the SUV limo before we climb in. Once seated inside, we turn up the dance music, pour a round of champagne, and toast to Paige.

We instruct the driver to take us to a club in Novi, so we have about forty-five minutes in the limo until we get there.

"This party is awesome. Thank you, London." Paige leans her head on my shoulder.

"You're so welcome. You know I love you."

"And I love you," she responds, her voice slightly slurred.

I make a mental note to watch her drink intake from here on out. No one wants to get sick on their birthday. I blame Kristyn's Jell-O shots. Those things are lethal.

As I sit here in this limo, surrounded by happiness and laughter, a huge amount of gratitude comes over me. I don't when it was that I started taking my life for granted. Maybe I always have. But I don't anymore. I now know how fortunate I am.

At the end of the day, I know I'll always have a small part of me that's materialistic and slightly shallow. Yet I realize that it isn't things that make one happy; it's people and the experiences shared with those people. Life is about those people one surrounds themselves with and the mutual love and respect that they share. And I'd have to say that I have a pretty amazing group of people in my corner.

NINE

Loïc

"In my life, there's always a falling ball.
I just hope I can catch it this time around."
—Loïc Berkeley

I wake with a start, yet again. Quickly sitting up, I hold my hands to my head, waiting for the dizziness to subside.

Another fucking nightmare.

At least London didn't have to witness this one. She went out with friends for Paige's birthday last night. I opted just to sleep in my own bed due to the fact that I have five a.m. PT this morning. Nothing says good morning like an intense workout before the sun even comes up.

Looking to the clock on my bedside table, the display reads *4:03*. My alarm was set to go off in a few minutes anyway. I turn the alarm switch to off and make my way toward the shower, anxious to get the nightmare sweat off of my body.

The constant nightmares are getting real old. I seem to be having more of them lately, and most of the time, they involve Sarah.

Stepping into the shower, I smile at the memory of London trying to get me to figure out what the pieces of artwork represented in California. I use her prompts and questions to try to figure out the dreams. They're similar to art in that way—using imagery to represent something else. Maybe if I could resolve the deep-seated issue that's causing them, I could make them stop.

After showering, I get dressed in my workout clothes, and all this time, the only explanation that I can come up with is that Sarah represents loss to me. She was someone I tried to hold on to but couldn't. I'm getting ready to leave for a war zone in a few days, and I desperately want to come home to London in a year, but I'm scared that it isn't going to happen. I can't pinpoint why, but every day that passes and brings me closer to leaving, that fear gets louder.

I know, more than anyone, that just because I want something to work doesn't mean that it will. I can want a life with London more than anything, but I'm far from guaranteed it. I just keep waiting for the ball to drop—and there will be a ball. In my life, there's always a falling ball. I just hope I can catch it this time around.

I grab my bag before exiting my room. I'm met in the hall by Cooper.

"Ready, man?" he asks.

"Yep."

We make our way out to my truck, and I drive toward the base. "So, tonight's the night, right?"

"Sure is."

"Your plans all set?" I ask.

"Yeah. It's not going to go down in the record books as the most romantic proposal of all time, but we're about to leave. I have limited time and options at this point, and I just want to ask her before I go."

"What's the plan again?"

"Well, when she comes home from work tonight, I'm going to have hundreds of candles and rose petals all over, lining a path to the living room, where I will be waiting to ask her. I'm also going to make her a romantic dinner—lobster Alfredo, her favorite. So, don't forget to be gone tonight." Cooper chuckles.

"No worries. I'll be at London's. Maggie's going to eat that shit up, dude. She's going to love it."

"I hope so."

"She will. I guarantee she'll be a blubbering mess. But, seriously, that girl would marry you if you put a ring in a Big Mac container and handed it to her. She doesn't care."

"Uh, a Big Mac? Why didn't I think of that?" Cooper asks sarcastically.

"Sorry, you'll have to go with your plan. I called the Big Mac box."

"Wow, never heard you even joke about getting married someday," Cooper says seriously.

I just shrug as a response.

I hear the warmth in Cooper's voice as he says, "I'm happy for you, man. London's great."

"Yeah, she is," I agree.

"Hey, baby." I find London sitting in her room, typing away on her laptop, obviously deep into one of her articles.

She looks up to me, and her eyes widen in surprise. "Hey! You got out early."

She stands from her desk chair as I reach her, and I pull her into a hug.

"What are you writing about?" I question, holding her in my arms.

"Well, actually, it's a great story. Remember a couple of weeks ago when I wrote about that three-legged dog named Scooter and how he showed up missing from that animal rescue farm down in Monroe?"

"Yeah?"

"Well," London says happily, "he was found!"

"Really?"

"Yes, he must have wandered off or something. They found him in the woods about a mile away from the farm. He had fallen in a hole and couldn't climb out. A little three-year-old boy was out on a walk with his grandma and actually heard him whimpering. They knew about the three-legged pup that'd been missing, so they drove him to the farm. But they loved the little pup so much that they're going to adopt him. Isn't that so sweet?"

"That is," I agree.

"Yeah, a photographer from work went out to the farm and snapped some pics of the little boy, his family, and the puppy. So, now, I just have to write the story to go along with the photos. I love writing these feel-good pieces."

"That's great, babe. I can't wait to read it." I smile down at my hot little journalist. Changing the subject, I ask, "How was Paige's birthday?"

"Oh, it was great. Dancing, drinks, all that jazz. I think she had fun." She places her palms on my face and pulls me into a kiss.

Her lips, as always, are perfect. Plump, sweet, and so kissable. I could get lost in her kisses.

I reluctantly pull away. "How are you feeling? You hungover?"

London scoffs, "Uh, no." She jovially pushes my chest away and reaches down to save whatever she was working on before shutting her laptop down. "Why do you ask?"

"I don't know. You went out drinking for Paige's birthday. I just figured it had gotten a little crazy." I shrug.

"Well, for your information, I do have some self-control." She pouts out her lips and narrows her eyes. "Plus, I didn't want to feel tired today. I don't want to waste any of these last few days with you by feeling icky, you know?"

"That's good because I have a surprise for you." My lips turn up in a smile.

"Oh, no. That look is never followed by anything good," she teases.

"Would you stop acting like everything we do is torture?" I chuckle. "You always protest, but then you end up having a great time. You know, I think you are addicted to complaining."

"I am not! I'm just not as outdoorsy as you." She turns her face, her gaze finding the window. "Plus, it's so cold outside," she says with a sigh. "You know I hate being cold."

"Well, suck it up, buttercup."

"All right." Her tone's resigned. "What should I wear for this surprise?"

"Something warm and comfortable, maybe stretchy."

"Stretchy? What are we doing?"

"You'll see. Just get ready." I grin, playfully shooing her away.

"Okay, okay. I have about five minutes of work to do on this article before I can send it in, and then I'm on it."

"An ice rink?" London asks as we pull into the Ann Arbor rink.

"Yeah. Since I'm going to be gone before the lakes freeze, I thought it would be fun to go ice-skating here."

"Hmm…interesting."

"Now, before you go complaining, just give it a chance."

We exit my truck and head toward the rink.

"It's fun, I promise. You'll get the hang of it relatively soon, and I'll hold your hand until you do, okay?"

"All right, I guess I can try," London says, not sounding too convinced.

"Thank you, babe. That's all I ask."

Once inside, we rent some skates and put them on.

"You know, they have these little walker-type things for kids just learning how to skate, but I don't think they have any tall enough for you," I say with a smirk.

"Ha-ha," she says, not sounding amused. "I think I'll be okay."

"There you go. You'll do great."

I hold London's hand as we step onto the ice. It's currently open skate, the rink is open for the public, but only two other people are on the ice along with us.

"So, I just move my feet?" she asks hesitantly.

"Yeah. You just kinda kick them back to propel you forward. Have you ever roller-skated? It's similar."

She lets go of my hand. "I think I'll try it on my own."

"You sure you don't want me to hold on to you for the first couple of laps? Falling on the hard ice hurts."

"I think I can do it," she says, releasing my hand.

I really wish she would let me help her. If she falls and gets a huge bruise, that'll be the end of ice-skating for us. She'll never let me hear the end of it.

"Okay."

She takes off on the ice, speeding around the oval rink. She skates with confidence and stability. I shake my head and chuckle. She can totally skate. I watch in shock as she skates backward, her arms out to the sides. She propels herself with her outer leg and then jumps, completing a midair spin, before landing on her feet.

What the…

Now, she's gliding across the ice on one foot, and her right foot is extended behind her as she leans forward, her arms back against her sides. She continues to skate around the ice, and all I can do is watch, my mouth agape, as she spins, twirls, and jumps. Her skills aren't equal to those of a professional skater, but they're way more than I can do, and it's a hell of surprise from what I assumed she would be able to do.

She slows until she's in the middle of the rink. Raising her arms above her head and crossing her feet, she ends in this fast spin that makes me dizzy as I watch. When she finishes spinning, she puts her arms out and bows in a curtsy.

She shoots me a knowing smirk, and I lose it, bending at the waist in laughter.

What did I just witness?

She skates over to me, a triumphant smile gracing her face. Her eyes shine with happiness.

She tilts her head to the side. "Did I do okay?" Her voice comes out hesitant, but I know it's the opposite of the way she's feeling.

I calm my laughter before saying, "What the hell was that?"

"Just ice-skating." She shrugs.

"Holy hell, London. You were doing jumps and spins and shit. Seriously...what did I miss?" I chuckle, shaking my head in disbelief.

"Oh, maybe I forgot to mention that I can skate?"

"Yeah, maybe you did. Though you can more than skate."

She claps her hands in front of her and lets out a giggle. "That was fun! The look on your face was priceless!"

"I bet it was." I grin. "I don't know if I've ever been more surprised in my life. So, really...what's the story?"

"Well, when I was little, I watched the Nagano Olympics with my mom, and let's just say that she really wanted me to be the next Tara Lipinski."

"Who's that?"

"She was an awesome figure skater that represented the United States."

"So, you took classes?"

"Yeah, I took lessons from about five years old until I was almost ten. I didn't have the drive to work hard enough to compete though. Plus, we moved all the time, and I always had to start fresh with a new coach. Right before my tenth birthday, I told my mom that I didn't want to do it anymore."

"Did you compete at all?"

"Like local stuff, nothing big."

"Wow. How did I not know this about you? Why didn't you ever say anything?"

London shrugs. "I don't know. I guess it just never came up. It wasn't a huge part of my life."

"It was five years of your life, London," I quip.

"I guess, but it was just skating to me. It was my mom's dream, but it wasn't mine."

"Well, regardless, it's pretty badass. I could never do that. And, now that I know you're comfortable on the ice, we're definitely going to have some ice hockey games in our future."

"Oh, crap. I should have just pretended to suck." She sighs.

"Would you stop?" I laugh. "Come on." I reach my hand out to hers. "Do you think you could skate on my level for a bit?"

She entwines her fingers in mine. "I suppose." She winks.

"What else don't I know about you?" I ask as we glide around the ice.

"I think that's all."

"I doubt it." I grin. "I think there's a lot that I still don't know about you, London, and I can't wait to discover it all."

She squeezes my hand in hers and turns her head to shoot me one of her stunning smiles. In this moment, I feel like there's nothing that could tear us apart. This love I have for her is so strong, and the way in which I adore her is so real that I'm pretty sure I would do just about anything to keep her forever.

TEN

London

"I can fall apart when he's gone.
But, right now, I just want to love him."
—London Wright

Fake green vines border the window, circling around it like an epic Pinterest fail. The bright sunlight streaming in accents the years of dust coating the leaves. Even from where we sit a few tables away the layer of gray is evident. I've never understood the point of plastic foliage. It surely doesn't make this place seem any more Italian, and apparently, it's difficult to keep clean. I briefly close my eyes and focus my attention back to my tablemates before I start to fixate over the hideous wallpaper that's covered in bright purple grapes. Senor Abelli is lucky that he's one hell of chef, or he'd be out of business with such atrocious decor.

"Let me see your ring again," I say excitedly to Maggie over the excessively loud ambiance music of this Italian restaurant.

She holds out her hand, and I stare at the gleaming diamond. It's a modest ring, maybe three-fourths of a carat on a simple platinum band. It's perfect for Maggie and Cooper. Staring at it makes me so ecstatic—for them, for love.

"I love it. It's so sparkly!" I tell her for what must be the fifth time.

"I know. David did such a good job at picking it out. I'm so happy."

Even though I know Cooper is his last name, it still catches me off guard when Maggie calls him by his first name, and I have to remind myself of who we're talking about.

"He did. I'm so happy for you. So, when do you think you'll get married?"

I hear a noise come from Cooper. He could be choking on his Coke or trying to suppress a laugh. I can't tell.

"Probably right after they get back. I'm going to plan the wedding while they're gone. Right, baby?" Maggie asks Cooper.

"Right, baby," he replies from across the table, shooting Loïc a lighthearted look.

We're having a last dinner out as a group. I love our little foursome and our weekly date night. I'm going to miss this. The guys leave in two days, so after dinner, Loïc's going to come back to my place where we are going to be snuggling in bed, among other activities, for the next thirty-six hours until he leaves on Friday morning.

We had a fantastic time with my family in California—like, the best—but ever since we got back, time has been moving at triple speed, and I hate it. I try not to think about Loïc leaving. I mean, I know he's going to, but I venture to remain in a state of denial. I can fall apart when he's gone. But, right now, I just want to love him and enjoy every second.

"So, what are your plans for tomorrow?" I ask Maggie and Cooper.

Maggie places her glass of red wine on the table. "David's family is throwing a full-day bon voyage celebration."

"It's more or less a day of drinking and shenanigans." Cooper chuckles.

"From what I've heard, your family sounds like a lot of fun." I grin.

"Oh, they are," Maggie agrees.

"You have three sisters, right, Cooper?" I ask, wanting to clarify the details of a conversation I had with him one of the first times I met him.

"Yep, I'm the youngest of four. We're basically all a year to eighteen months apart, starting with Kate—the oldest—then Becca, Jen, and finally, me. Kate has two kids; little Emma is four, and Jack is two. Becca's pregnant with her first, and Jen might never settle down. We're not sure. But Becca's and Kate's husbands are awesome. The whole family is loud and fun."

"Yeah, and David's the loudest," Maggie adds.

"Well, when you're born after three incredibly needy sisters, you've got to fight for your place in the food chain. I did that by being obnoxiously vocal and annoying—or so they tell me. But everyone took the day off tomorrow, and we're just going to spend the day together. My dad will cook some good food. Mom will be scurrying around, making sure everyone has everything they need. I'm sure we'll be playing some games. It will be a great day."

"It will be." Maggie looks to Cooper with a hint of sorrow in her eyes before her lips turn up into a smile. "I love David's family. I definitely got lucky in the in-law department."

"You two are welcome to come hang out." Cooper motions his finger between Loïc and me. "My family is dying to meet you, London. They want to meet the girl who finally got under Loïc's skin." He chuckles. "Maggie's family's coming for part of the day, too."

"Aw…we would, but—"

"We've got plans," Loïc finishes my thought.

I smile warmly toward him. I know that he is looking forward to our marathon of alone time just as much as I am.

"We'll make it for your welcome-home party. How's that?" I ask Cooper.

"That's cool," he answers before shoving a huge forkful of noodles into his mouth.

"So, let's talk wedding plans!" I exclaim with sincere excitement. There's nothing more fun than planning an amazing party. I think I got my love of event-planning from my mom. "What are you thinking so far?" I ask Maggie.

"You know, you two are going to have a year to get together and discuss the wedding," Cooper states.

"We sure are, but there's no time like the present, right, baby?" Maggie asks.

"Right, baby," Cooper answers with what I think is a bit of a forced smile.

I look to Loïc, and he's just taking the whole scene in, a slight grin gracing his face.

Sometimes, like now, when I look to him, I can see the wheels turning in his beautiful brain. I can almost see his thoughts racing through his mind. Evident by the smile on his face, I know that they're positive ones.

I also know that isn't always the case.

My guy, he's so stoic at times. There are moments when he has a far off stare, and I'm almost certain he's remembering something troubling. He's pretty good at sharing with me. He's opened up so much over the past six months. But, still…what I wouldn't give to be able to read his thoughts.

For all he's shared with me about his tortured past and horrible experiences, I have a feeling that there's so much more he hasn't. Every now and then, when I think about the parts of his past that he hasn't confided in me, I get nervous. A small voice tells me, it's the secrets one buries the deepest that have the power to destroy them. And though I love to be right, when it comes to that, I hope I'm wrong.

After we get back from the restaurant, Loïc and I shower and climb into bed.

"Do you remember that flight we were on together back in June?" Loïc asks.

"Of course. How could I forget?" I answer playfully.

"Remember how annoying you were?"

"Hey!" I hit him on his chest. "Well, I couldn't have been that annoying because you kissed me out of the blue. Aw…that was our first kiss. Is that why you thought about that flight?"

"No, though that was a definite highlight. I was actually thinking about your Twenty Questions game and how you were so irritatingly curious and persistent and wanted to be all up in my business." He chuckles.

"I couldn't help it. When I see something I want, I can be very persistent."

"That you can." He's quiet for a moment. "That's what I want to do tonight."

"What?"

"I want to play a version of your game. I want to learn as much about you as I can before I go. While I'm over there, I want to have a plethora of information to choose from when I think about you."

"Aw, that's sweet. But don't you already know everything about me?" I turn my face to the side to stare into his blue depths.

Loïc lies on his side, his head propped up by his hand, as he faces me. "I know a lot but definitely not everything. I had no idea that you were a trained figure skater."

"A minor oversight." I snuggle into his side.

"Well, there are other things I don't know. For example, um…what is your favorite childhood memory?"

"That's a hard one!" I exclaim. "Let me think. Oh, I got it. Okay, so once, when I was about ten and Georgia was eight, we were staying in this rental house up in the hills, by Gatlinburg. I don't remember why we were staying there. It might have been a vacation, or more than likely, my dad had business nearby. It was spring— beginning of April, I think. There was a late-season snowstorm, tons of snow…like, up to my knees. We lost power, and cars couldn't go up or down the hill with all the snow. The power was out for almost two days, and my dad couldn't work during that time. Also, the catering company couldn't get up the hill to bring us meals. So, for two days, we ate random snacks from the pantry—chips, Teddy Grahams, dry cereal, stuff like that. Dad made a fire in the fireplace, and the four of us played board games all night by the light and warmth of the fire. We had an epic Monopoly battle going on. Georgia ended up winning, but I'm almost positive she snuck some money." I smile, thinking about that night. "It was such a wonderful couple of days. I had uninterrupted time with my entire family. I don't remember ever laughing so much or having that much fun. It's something so simple, but that's what stands out to me as the best memory."

"I love that story," Loïc answers.

"What's yours?"

"I think it was probably the last Christmas that my grandparents were able to come over from England. I was five. I don't remember everything about the day, honestly. I was so young, but bits and pieces come back to me from time to time. I remember my mom was often sad, but she was especially happy that day. I recall my granddad being really funny. He was always doing weird things.

"I remember my dad and Nan working together in the kitchen, making Christmas dinner. They were belting out Beatles songs. Even at that age, I knew that neither of them could carry a tune, but it didn't matter; it was so fun to listen to them. They both loved to laugh a lot.

"I don't even recall what presents I got that day. Legos maybe? But the thing that stands out the most about it was just the feeling of complete joy. We were all so happy. After my parents died, that feeling of joy got me through a lot of hard nights. I drew on that memory to give me strength. Over the years, the details have faded, but the immense sense of happiness never has."

"That's beautiful, Loïc," I say in a whisper. "It's kind of neat that the central focus of both of our memories is family and the feeling of happiness. I guess it shows what's important in life, doesn't it?"

"Yeah, I suppose it does," Loïc says thoughtfully.

"Oh, I have an idea!" I grab Loïc's arm and squeeze with excitement.

"Yeah?" He looks amused.

"How about, while you're gone, we can play a really long Twenty Questions game? So, every email I send, I'll ask you a question, and when you respond, you'll answer it and then ask me a question. Of course, when you ask a question, you have to answer it as well. It will be fun, something to look forward to, you know?"

"That sounds great," he agrees. "Actually, that will be cool because a lot of what goes on over there, I won't be able to share with you. So, now, I'll have something to write to you besides *I love you* and *I'm still alive.*"

My eyes open wide as I gasp. "Don't even joke about that, Loïc. That's not funny."

"I didn't mean it to be funny, London, but things happen sometimes. It's a possibility." His face wears an expression of remorse.

My eyes fill with tears. "It's not. You'll be fine. You'll be back, but you have to think positively. Promise me that you won't say anything like that again. I mean, I could walk out my front door and get hit by a car tomorrow, but I'm not going to wake up and say, *Hope I don't die today.*"

"Yeah, but my situation is a little different."

"Maybe, but can we pretend it's not? Let's just look forward to when you come back, safe and sound, okay? I can't handle thinking about the alternative. To me, there is no alternative. There can't be one for you either. Got it? Promise me that you'll come back to me."

"Okay."

"Thank you," I sigh as I wrap my arms around his back and nuzzle into his chest. It's not the most profound promise, but I'll take it.

ELEVEN

London

"This pain isn't exclusive to me, but it aches as if it is."
—London Wright

"I love you," I say, forcing my voice to be steady with strength that I didn't know I had.

"I know, and I love you, London—more than you'll ever know. I'm not good with words." He pauses, letting out a strained sigh. *"And this good-bye stuff is so new and hard. I want to tell you all the right things…and I just…"* His voice trails off as he grabs the back of his neck. His eyes close, and he lets his head fall back until his face points toward the cloudy sky.

"Hey…" I place the palm of my hand against his abdomen.

He lowers his gaze to meet mine.

"First, you are amazing with words, much more so than you give yourself credit for."

He smiles, but it doesn't reach his eyes. They emit so much sadness, but I know he's trying hard to be strong for me.

"We knew this was coming, right?" I say more to myself than him. "You're going to go and do your job and come back to me. You're going to be fine. I'm going to work and go on with life while you're gone. I'm going to be fine. We're going to be okay, Loïc…I promise you. This isn't forever. In fact, in the story of our lives, this will be a very small chapter."

I wrap my arms around his waist and rest my cheek against his chest, absorbing as much of his warmth as possible. "You're off to do something noble and great. You have an important job, and I couldn't be prouder of you. I'm so happy we found each other, Loïc. I love you so much. I'm going to write to you every day. We're going to be okay," I repeat. "We're going to make it."

"I love you, London. I'll email back and call you as often as I can."

Pulling my face back, I peer up to him. "It's just a year. We totally got this." I force a grin.

He nods. "We got this."

He bends as I rise up on my toes. Our lips meet, and it's perfection. Loïc's wrong when he says that he's not good with words because he's said some pretty swoonworthy things to me in the time that I've known him. But the thing is that he wouldn't even have to because no one has ever communicated more love through a kiss than Loïc. Truthfully, he doesn't have to utter a syllable because this kiss, his lips, his passion say everything that I could hope to hear.

He left.

Eight hours ago, I kissed Loïc for what was the last time for a while—for about three hundred sixty-four days actually, if we're lucky.

I watched as he boarded the bus with his duffel bag thrown over his shoulder. I stood with Maggie in the parking lot of their military base as a hundred or so other men dressed in camouflage boarded buses as well. I was surrounded by people—wives, mothers, sisters, girlfriends, fathers, brothers, and children. Many were crying with looks of sadness, fear, and heartbreak haunting their faces. Others wore brave expressions in hopes of giving their soldiers strength on their journey. I was in that group. I waved and blew kisses with a strained smile as the military procession pulled away.

Long after the busses were out of sight, my hand continued to move back and forth in front of me, the pained smile frozen to my face. Eventually, I dropped it. Sighing, I gave Maggie a quick hug, and I left.

Now, I'm sitting, cross-legged, on my couch, where I've been sitting for the better part of the day, feeling numb.

It's been mere hours since I've seen Loïc, yet the gravity of a year of longing is weighing down on my heart, causing a pain I've never known.

I know that I'm not the first to see their soldier off on deployment. I realize that countless wives have said good-bye to their husbands, the fathers of their children. This pain isn't exclusive to me, but it aches as if it is.

I ignored the impending sorrow that the enormity of this reality was sure to bring for so long, not wanting to spend a second of my time left with Loïc feeling down. But it's here now, and I must face the next year without him. I just don't know what to do with myself or how to make this hollowness in my chest go away.

My cell vibrates next to my leg. My hand springs for it, causing it to fumble in my grasp. I take a calming breath and hold the phone steady. Loïc's name flashes across the screen along with one of my favorite pictures of the two of us.

I quickly swipe the screen to answer. "Hey." My voice sounds relatively okay, not hinting to the internal mess that I am.

"Hey, babe. Miss me yet?"

"Very much," I answer honestly. "Did you just get there?"

The busses took the guys to a National Guard base in Columbus, Ohio, where they will leave from tomorrow.

"A few hours ago. We've been debriefing and getting everything ready to leave tomorrow. We're done for the rest of the night though."

"Oh, that's good. What are you gonna do?"

"I'm going to go out with Sarah and Cooper, maybe dinner and bowling or something low-key."

There's a buzzing in my ears from all the blood rushing to my head. I didn't hear everything Loïc just said, seeing that I kind of blanked out after I heard the word *Sarah*. I'm pretty sure, if one's head could explode from fury, my brain matter would already be decorating these walls.

"Sarah?" I say as steadily as possible.

"Oh, yeah. She drove up here for the day to surprise me. She wanted to say good-bye in person."

Oh, I bet she did.

"I didn't realize that you could have visitors tonight. I would have flown down to spend the evening with you." My lip quivers, and I have to stop the impending waterworks.

"It's okay, babe. It's not really common practice to have visitors here. Sarah just showed up, and it kinda all worked out because we finished up early."

I sigh into the phone, at a loss for what to say.

"I miss you, too, London," Loïc says sweetly.

"Yeah? Like, a lot?"

"An insane amount."

A small smile spreads across my face. "I miss you like crazy, too."

"Remember, everything will be okay…right?" he says, trying to reassure me.

"I know."

"All right, well, we're heading out. I'll call you tomorrow morning before we leave."

"Okay, I love you."

"I love you, too," he says before the line goes dead.

I hold my cell phone in my lap and just stare at it. I'm so lost already, and my journey has barely begun. *How will I ever find my way?*

I raise my head when I hear Paige enter the living room. She's just getting back from work.

Placing her leather laptop bag on the chair, she looks to me with a worried expression. "Are you okay?"

I shake my head, biting my lip to stop it from trembling.

"Do you want to talk about it?"

I shrug, my eyes filling with unshed tears.

"Do you know what we need?" The question is rhetorical, so she continues, "We need a good old-fashioned cry session. I'm talking about snot-dripping, chest-heaving, shrieking-sobs ugly cry. Then, I'm going to pick up dinner—your choice—and of course, get some Ben and Jerry's Chubby Hubby for you." She winks. "Then, we're going to have a romantic movie marathon and stuff our faces while we cry until we can't cry anymore." She taps her lips with her finger. "We should start with *The Notebook*. That's a guaranteed ugly cry right there. Sound good?"

I nod marginally as the tears start falling, months of repressed worry needing to escape. Paige sits next to me on the couch and wraps her arms around me. As I lean my head against her shoulder, the waterworks really come. My back shakes with sobs as all my fears and sadness fall onto Paige's fancy new business suit.

I don't know how long I cry, but when the tears cease, my throat feels raw, and my face is hot and itchy.

I sit up and stare at the huge pond of tears and snot that I left on Paige's shoulder and chest. I drag my arm across my nose. "I'm sorry, Paige. I think I ruined your outfit."

She waves me off. "You know what they say. *A watched pot never boils.* It will be fine after a quick trip to the dry cleaner."

I wipe my wet face with my shirt before I start to laugh.

"What?" Paige asks.

"Sometimes, you are the smartest person I know, and then other times…you make absolutely no sense. What would I do without you?" I say with a chuckle.

"Well, clearly, you'd be lost." Paige winks. "Listen, you go shower while I pick up supplies. What do you feel like tonight? Chinese?"

"No, I think pizza. You know that deep dish one with the extra buttery crust from our favorite place? Oh, and don't forgot the extra ranch to dip it in."

"Nice. We're not playing around tonight!" Paige looks down at her attire. "So, I'm going to change out of these snot rags really quick, and then I'll head out. When I come back, I want you showered, in your comfiest clothes, and ready for a night of feeling sorry for ourselves. Got it?"

"Got it." I nod, feeling more human than I have all day.

I dip the garlic-buttered goodness into the container of homemade ranch and practically moan when it hits my mouth. I might have to go on a walk or something tomorrow to counter my calorie intake tonight, but it's so worth it.

Paige and I sit atop my bed in our jammies with the menu screen for *The Notebook* playing on repeat on the TV screen.

Paige takes a sip of wine before asking, "So, Sarah's there?"

"I know," I sigh dejectedly. "I hate it. I know I shouldn't, but I do."

"I get it." Paige gives me a knowing nod.

"Right? I mean, yeah, they're friends, family, whatever...but she's a woman. There's history there. I hate that his last night stateside is being spent with her. It should be with me. It just pisses me off." I shake my head. "I'm not mad at Loïc. First, he didn't know she was coming, and second...he doesn't get it anyway. But Sarah is another story. She should know better."

"Exactly. She definitely broke some sort of girl code by showing up there. I don't care what their history is," Paige agrees. "You don't think anything will happen, do you?"

Biting my lip, I ponder for a moment. "No, I don't. I can't see Loïc cheating on me. I believe in what we have, and I trust that he cares for Sarah only as a friend. But that doesn't mean I'm not jealous as hell that she gets to be with him tonight, and I don't. I told you what her last name is, right?"

"No." Paige shakes her head. "I don't know her last name."

"It's Berkeley!" I almost shout.

"What?" Paige shrieks.

"Yeah, last week, he got a text from her, and I saw her name come up on his phone as *Sarah Berkeley*. I questioned him about it, and he said that, when they first ran away together, she told him that she was taking his last name. I guess she hated hers or had bad memories from it or something. Loïc doesn't even know her original last name."

"So, she, like, legally changed it or something?"

"I guess." I shrug. "I think it's weird. Their closeness already makes me uncomfortable, and to top it off, they share a last name."

"I suppose you could just think of her as his sister. I mean, siblings share last names, right?"

"Yeah, I didn't think about it like that. He does say she's like a sister to him."

"There you go! Well, anyway…I'm sure today will be the worst of it for you. You'll get better at being apart from Loïc. You'll find a new normal where you won't miss him so much."

"I sure hope so. I can't take too many more days like today."

"Plus, maybe this time apart will even strengthen your relationship. You know what they say. *Absence makes the heart grow fonder.*"

I grin. "Aw, look at you, making all sorts of sense."

"When I've got it, I've got it." Paige looks smug.

"You're such a dork." I giggle.

TWELVE

Loïc

"One week down, and fifty-one more to go."
—*Loïc Berkeley*

A week of plane travel, a stop off in Qatar, and a short three-day layover in Kuwait, and we've finally arrived at our final destination—Bagram Air Base in Afghanistan. Cooper and I always say that the Army doesn't get anywhere fast.

I'm exhausted, but the traveling hasn't been that bad. When we're not sleeping, we're shooting the shit with the rest of the guys in our deployment unit. I've been deployed with many of the same guys before, so it's cool to see them again and hear what they've been up to since our last tour in Iraq.

As far as bases go, Bagram's not bad. It's the size of a small city. It's basically sectioned off in two halves—the west and east side. Our unit is stationed on the west side, as is most of the Army and Navy. The east side mainly houses the flyers, the Air Force units. It has several huge mess halls—where I'm hoping they have decent food—a couple of gyms, a recreation building, and decent living quarters.

After checking in with command and grabbing our issued supplies, Cooper and I grab our duffels and head to our designated living quarters. The buildings are large wooden rectangular cubes. We walk down the dimly lit narrow hall. The plywood beneath our boots creak with each step. Toward the end of the hallway, I spot a white piece of paper taped to a wooden door with *Berkeley* scrawled across it. The door to the right of mine has the same welcome sign but with *Cooper* written on it.

"Home sweet home," Cooper says with an air of sarcasm.

"Yep," I sigh.

"Chow in an hour?" Cooper says as he enters his room.

"Okay," I respond before my door closes behind me.

We're fortunate. Because of our rank and jobs, we get our own places. Granted, the room isn't much more than a box. It's as wide as my bed; the head and foot of the twin bed touches each opposing wall. To the right of the bed are a small desk and chair. There's enough space to set my trunk of stuff beside the foot of the bed, and that's about it. But it beats having a roommate any day.

The first thing I do is pull out the laptop I brought from home. It's a few years old and enclosed in a durable silver case. I brought it for mission-related work, like writing reports and doing research. But, of course, its most important function will be emailing and Skyping with London back home. Having Internet at this place, which exists in a valley at the base of a section of the magnificent Hindu Kush mountain range, is a feat in itself. I wouldn't think they could get reliable signals here, but thankfully for me, they do—or at least most of the time. I've heard the Internet here is spotty—going in and out throughout the day—but it's better than not having it at all.

It's been seven days exactly since I've seen London, and sure enough, when I finally sit down in front of my wobbly little desk and log into my Gmail, I find seven emails from London, entitled *Question 1* through *Question 7*.

I open the oldest email first.

To: Loïc Berkeley

From: London Wright

Subject: Question 1—Last Meal

Hey, babe. So, I saw you this morning, which means that you haven't even technically left yet. But I promised that I would write you once a day, so here I am, writing you.

Let me start out by saying that I already miss you like crazy. Like, I might have turned into a crazy person in a matter of ten hours minus Loïc. Completely insane. *Loco en la cabeza*. That means crazy in the head. It's, like, the one phrase I remember from high school Spanish. I mean, just the mere thought of you being gone is driving me crazy.

What am I actually going to do when it's been days or months versus hours?

I'm being a total bitch, right? I mean, you're the one being shipped off to some Third World terrorist country, and I'm the one sitting here, feeling sorry for myself. I'm selfish. What can I say? You already know that's a major flaw of mine. ;-)

I know I tried to be all positive before you left. "Oh, it's just a year! A year is nothing!" Blah, blah, blah. Well, I'm calling total BS. A year is a very long freaking time, and I hate it already.

Don't take this to mean I'm not going to wait or anything silly like that. You're stuck with me forever, Loïc Berkeley.

I just recently decided—like, three minutes ago when I started typing this letter—that we should be completely honest with each other while you're gone. I don't know if that's a good idea or not. I could just be speaking out of my ass. But I was thinking that, maybe if we're open and honest with everything, including our fears, then we can help each other get over them or at least talk about them, you know?

Putting your feelings out in the open is supposed to help. Total transparency, right?

So, here I am, telling you that I love you and I miss you and that this year without you is going to totally blow— and you haven't even left US soil yet! Ugh.

So, question 1, if you were dying—like, let's say you were about to be electrocuted for a crime—what would you request as your last meal?

My answer is shrimp pad thai from this new place in Ann Arbor. Paige brought home takeout, and I'm telling you, these noodles are to freaking die for. Like, so good. When you get back in a year, we are going there, so you can see for yourself.

I love you so much.

Love,

London

I shake my head, a huge smile on my face. She is one of a kind; that's for sure. I start typing.

To: London Wright

From: Loïc Berkeley

Subject: Re: Question 1—Last Meal

London, baby,

First, I don't know what about your email is more disturbing—that it sounded a lot like a Dear John letter (thanks for clarifying that it wasn't) or that your question involves me dying (not cool, given my current situation). How's that for transparency? Lol. Seriously, your level of tact, or lack thereof, is kind of a flaw, babe. You're lucky I love you so much.

And selfish? Maybe a tad, but at the same time, you're incredibly giving to the ones you love the most. You love fiercely, and that is one of my favorite things about you. You're intense and real. You don't sugarcoat anything, and for some odd reason, I find that hot as hell. I love your sass and your humor. I just love you, and I, too, miss the hell out of you already.

A year is a long time, but it'll get easier, right?

Not much going on here. Just arrived to the base where we'll be for a while and getting settled in.

Missing you. Loving you.

Cooper says hi, and he wants to make sure you're keeping Maggie company while we're gone. He also says that his favorite meal is a big, ole juicy medium-rare rib eye with a side of buttery au gratin potatoes and those cheesy biscuits from Red Lobster.

If you're wondering whether I asked him for his answer, that would be a solid no. He's just a nosy dick, who's reading over my shoulder. Apparently, he can't even stay away from me for a solid hour. He might be a stage-four clinger. Let's hope it doesn't escalate to stage five.

He's now saying that he's not a dick, but I'd have to disagree.

As far as my answer to your question goes, I'm going to have to say fish and chips—and not the American version, the UK version. One of the last places

I remember my dad taking me to was an English pub in South Carolina where he had to do some business. I drove there with him from Mississippi for a weekend, and we happened upon this pub. It was owned by an older guy with an accent that sounded just like my granddad's. My dad ordered us each fish and chips, and I remember that being the most delicious meal I'd ever had. I've never had fish and chips like it since. Maybe none other can compare because that meal is glorified in my head with extra doses of nostalgia and years of building it up. But if I were dying, I would want that meal again, and I would want it to taste the way it did in my memories.

So, how is this whole question thing going to work? Because, now, I have six more emails to respond to before I can ask my question. So, let's do this. Feel free to write me as much as you want, but you can only ask one question, and you can't ask another one until I write back with a question.

So, in a few minutes, after I get done responding to your other questions, I'm going to ask you question 8, and then you respond with 9, so I'll be even, and you're odd—in more ways than one, I might add. ;-)

I love you, babe.

Love,

Loïc

I quickly respond to the other emails with my answers only and then type out the question eight email before closing my laptop.

"Dude, seriously. We've basically just been on each other's asses for the past week, and you don't want an hour to yourself?" I look to Cooper, who's sprawled out on my bed, looking at the ceiling.

"Nah." He sits up. "I was bored," he says as way of an explanation.

"Didn't you want to write to Maggie?"

"I'll write her when we get back from dinner. We're eight and a half hours ahead, so that makes it nine thirty in the morning there. She's working today. She's not going to have time to check her emails until she gets off at seven tonight, her time. Right?"

I nod. "Yeah, I suppose you're right."

"What are the chances you suppose they'll be serving authentic English fish and chips and excellently prepared rib eyes?" he asks as we exit my room.

"I'm going to say slim to none." I chuckle.

"Damn, I'm hungry for a good steak now, thanks to you," he huffs.

"Well, it was your dumbass that insisted on being nosy."

"Eh, true. What can I say, Lieutenant Berkeley? I miss you when we're apart," he says with a voice rich in mock adoration.

"You're an idiot." I laugh.

"I plead the fifth. But, seriously, this food had better be edible, or it's going to be a long-ass year."

"Isn't that the truth?"

We walk in comfortable silence the rest of the way to the mess hall, which is a few blocks from our living quarters. Thoughts of London fill my head with each step.

One week down, and fifty-one more to go.

THIRTEEN

London

"I want to reach into the computer and hug him—
my wounded, brave, sexy warrior."
—London Wright

The red digital numbers on my bedside table shine brightly in the dark room. *Noon. Wow, I was out.*

It seems like a minute has passed since my head hit my pillow at three a.m. Paige and I went out last night to celebrate a new account she was given at work. Apparently, it's a hugely successful client and a detailed project for them to give to someone who's only been with the company for several months.

I don't understand all of Paige's marketing lingo, but the bottom line was that it called for a celebration. The Friday night bar scene in Ann Arbor didn't let us down, and I actually feel pretty good for how much I drank.

I roll out of bed and pull open my dark curtains to let in some light. Every branch of the tree outside my window is covered with snow. Actually, everything outside is covered in a blanket of white. We must have gotten a good eight inches or so overnight. I'll agree with Loïc; winter can be so beautiful. I just wish it weren't so cold. A momentary pang aches in my chest because Loïc missed the first big snowfall of the year. Then again, I suppose he's going to miss them all, isn't he?

I'm sure if he were here, we'd already be dressed in snow gear and out sledding or skiing or some other torturous event like that.

Exiting my room, I'm met with Paige in the hallway, and by the look of her bed head and puffy eyes, she just woke up as well.

"Did you see it snowed?" I ask.

"Yeah, so pretty," she says with a yawn.

"I need coffee," I say as I head into our kitchen. "French vanilla?"

"Sounds good."

I grab the bag of vanilla-flavored beans and grind up enough for Paige and me, and I start the pot.

"Oh! We have Mexican leftovers!" I practically cheer as I peer into the refrigerator for something to eat for breakfast.

"Oh, yes!" Paige yells behind me. "Why is it that Mexican food tastes so good after a night of drinking?"

"I don't know, but it really does." I pull off the cardboard tops and place the aluminum tins of goodness into the toaster oven to warm.

After a few minutes, we take our coffees and warmed leftovers to the dining room table.

"What do you want to do today?" Paige stuffs her mouth full of some rice.

"Well, I desperately need to finish my Christmas shopping. I'm glad that I sent Loïc a care package last week because, at this rate, he's not going to get his Christmas package until mid-January."

"Are you kidding? At only eight days away, your family will be lucky to get their presents on time." She chuckles.

"I know. I'm so behind, but I really don't want to be out driving in this snow. That's, like, a guaranteed accident right there."

"I bet there are some online stores that still offer rush shipping," Paige offers.

"Good call! Let's online shop today and then start a new show on Netflix," I say through a mouthful of chicken fajita.

"It's a plan."

After we've finished eating, I make myself presentable, meaning I wash my face and brush my hair and teeth. I quickly throw on a winter coat and some boots.

"Where are you going?" Paige asks when she sees me leaving the house.

"I'm going to go take some selfies with the snow, so I can email them to Loïc. He loves that crap."

"So, you're going to pretend to be out, enjoying the winter wonderland, when, in fact, you're going to be out there for less than two minutes?"

"Exactly," I beam, pretty proud of my plan.

"You're crazy." Paige chuckles to herself before taking a sip of coffee.

"Hey, I'm not going to lie to him, but if he assumes that I'm being outdoorsy, then who am I to tell him differently?" I shrug. Turning, I head out the front door.

After a minute and a half, I'm back inside. "I'm going to be in my room, emailing Loïc and then shopping. We can start our show in a couple of hours, okay?"

"Sounds good. I'm going to catch up with our favorite celeb BFFs," Paige says as she sprawls out on the couch with a stack of this week's gossip magazines.

Once in my room, I start up my laptop.

I'm thrilled when there's an email waiting for me. Loïc's been able to write every day since he arrived at Bagram. He's warned me that some of his jobs will take him away from base for a few days, so he won't be able to write then. But, for now, he can.

To: London Wright

From: Loïc Berkeley

Subject: Question 14

Hey, babe. To answer your last question...HOW DO YOU EXPECT ME TO ANSWER IT? Lol.

I can't possibly pick my favorite time having sex with you. Yes, the closet at the benefit was HOT, so that's a good choice. But there have been so many! Lake Michigan? The Mexican restaurant? The countless times in your bed? Shower sex? I mean...how am I supposed to choose? Seriously? They've all been perfection. You know my favorite thing in the world is being inside you, baby. Hard, fast, slow, rough, wet—I love it all.

BUT, if I must answer you, then I would have to say my favorite time was the first time because it only took once to know that my life would never be the same from that point forward. That's some romantic shit right there, but I mean it. ;-)

Not much going on here. Military stuff. I did beat Cooper by 2 seconds in our mile race, which is pretty awesome. He's being a baby and saying that he tripped on the gravel, so it doesn't count. But I say that I beat him fair and square. He's always been a whiner. ;-)

I hope you're doing well, babe. I think about you nonstop. I'm actually quite pathetic with the amount of time I spend thinking about you. I think I might be addicted. It's weird, missing someone here. I've always only had Cooper, and he's been with me on deployments, so it didn't really matter. This is my first taste of truly missing someone who's alive and well yet...so out of my reach. It's kind of a cruel form of torture.

I love you.

So, question 14, where's a place you've never been that you'd love to visit?

My answer is London, England. The reasons are pretty obvious, but I think I've put off my trip there long enough. I need to see all the places that my dad used to tell me about. I need to look up my grandparents and ask them why they never came for me. I think, to completely put my past behind me, I need the closure—for good or bad—that their answers will bring.

If you want to know the truth, I've been too much of a coward up until this point to find out. The little boy inside me was too scared to know because, sometimes, the truth hurts more than one is capable of dealing with. A long time ago, I started using hate to cover up my hurt. But I think I'm finally ready and able to go there.

You and your love have helped me more than you will ever know. Your love gives me the strength to do things that I never thought I could.

I love you, London, baby.

Love,

Loïc

His email makes me hurt. I want to reach into the computer and hug him—my wounded, brave, sexy warrior.

To: Loïc Berkeley

From: London Wright

Subject: Question 15

Loïc, you are brave, and you have more courage than anyone I've ever known. Maybe I helped you see that in yourself, but it was there all along.

I'm glad you want to go to London. I think that will help you so much. There has to be a reason for everything. And, if there's not a good one, you'll be fine with that, too.

You have conquered more true heartaches and obstacles than any one person ever should. But you're still here. You're strong. You're perfect... cracks and all.

And I love you more than I ever thought possible.

To answer your question, if I could go any place right now that I've never been...well, it'd surely be Bagram, Afghanistan. No questions asked. I've heard that not only is the hottest man alive there, but that the mountains are pretty, too. :-)

I woke up to the most beautiful snow today and immediately thought of you.

I'm attaching some pics of me and said snow. I was going to let you believe what you want, but in full disclosure, I must admit that I was only outside for, like, a minute. You know, if you were here, you would have us gallivanting all over the great state of Michigan, doing all sorts of outdoor activities. But I decided to slowly build up my endurance so that I can hang with you next winter. And, yes, a minute was my limit. I have some work to do. ;-) Regardless, the pictures are cute, and I hope they bring a smile to your face.

I'm about to do some online shopping and hang with Paige for the day. I hope whatever you are doing, you are safe and happy. I love you.

Question 15: What's your favorite animal?

Mine's a dog. I think they are so adorable and sweet. Growing up, I always wanted a puppy, but my dad is allergic, so it was never an option. Just FYI, someday, you and I are going to get a puppy together. Maybe, if you're lucky, I'll let you name him. Of course, I'd have to agree on it. ;-)

Love you,

London

FOURTEEN

Loïc

"It's hard to risk your life and to see your brothers lose their lives for a cause that's often hard to find."
—Loïc Berkeley

I'm lacing up my tennis shoes when I hear the first blast—a mortar. I'd be surprised if that one even made it inside the wire, the area protected by our troops. Mortar attacks are at least a weekly occurrence. The Taliban set up these Chinese rockets quite often, usually on a timer so that they're not still in the area when the rockets shoot off. At least half of the time, they detonate outside the wire, but they do land on base as well.

I jump when a second boom from a rocket sounds, this time close enough that the cheap wood beneath my feet trembles.

Shit.

I lunge toward the exit and swing open my door just as the base's sirens go off, warning us to take shelter.

Cooper comes flying out of his room at the same time, his hair a disheveled mess and his eyes still puffy with sleep.

"Hell of a wake-up call!" he yells to me over the hums of disarray.

We sprint out of the building.

Another explosion, and this one is deafening, hitting the sleeping quarters about fifty yards to my left. My hands instinctively cover my ears that are now ringing as I turn my face away from the blast that has sent wooden fragments racing through the air. We run faster. In a matter of seconds, along with everyone else housed in this section of the base, we're safe within the bunker.

"Kent!" Cooper shouts to one of our brothers whose room in the building was just demolished by a mortar. "Did everyone get out?"

"Still missing Carter!" Kent yells back as he continues to scan the space, an unsettling fear present in his eyes.

Carter's just a kid—eighteen, I think. He's real funny. This is his first tour, and he's already well liked on base. He's one of those guys who gets along with everyone. As one of the youngest guys on base, he fills the role of everyone's little goofball brother. A pang hits my chest as I immediately start searching the faces in the tight space, praying to see Carter's mischievous grin.

"Oh, Carter was switched to night watch," a brother from Kent's unit answers.

I stop scanning to listen.

"When?" Kent asks.

"Last night was his first night. He wasn't back from watch yet when the mortar hit," the soldier responds.

The collective sigh of relief coming from the men in the cement bunker can almost be heard over the chaos sounding outside.

My rapidly beating heart calms as we all hunker down and wait. The atmosphere's calmer now that all of our brothers are accounted for. A few more mortars go off, but they're farther away.

After a period of time goes by without any blasts, the siren rings, informing us that we can leave the bunker.

"Well, all right. Ready for some chow?" Cooper asks me as we walk past the now demolished living quarters of Kent and his unit.

"Yeah," I respond before nodding toward the shattered pile of wood and debris. "That sucks."

"Sure does," Cooper agrees. "Glad everyone got out before it hit though."

"Let's hope they're serving something better today than that shitty excuse for French toast," I huff out.

The quality of food offered at the chow hall is hit or miss, depending on which contractor is providing the food that day. Yesterday, they served French toast that was coated in raw eggs, like they hadn't even known to cook that shit.

"Or that slimy sausage." Cooper shudders. "Greasy, I can handle. Slimy, no way."

"Agreed."

"Well, at least we'll have steak and lobster tonight. Another week down," Cooper states.

I nod.

Another week down.

Every Friday, the dining hall serves steak and lobster for dinner. It's shitty, but crappy steak and lobster is better than none. Cooper and I count down how many weeks we've been here by how many steak and lobster dinners we've had. It's amusing how much time we spend figuring out new ways to count down the time until we leave.

133

After a breakfast free of slime and raw eggs, we head to our mission prep brief, which lasts hours longer than it should. The topics of discussion veer drastically from the agenda that pertains to our upcoming mission. We go over everything from supply issues and lost weapons to Baker's cheating whore wife and how to support him here as he deals with the news. At times, being in the military is like having a crucial role in the operation of a badass fine-tuned machine designed for greatness, and other times, it's like having a role in a dramatic soap opera with a horrible plotline.

Yet, even as I sit here, cringing inside, wondering how Baker could have ever married a tramp who would sleep with their babysitter's son—who is a senior in high school—only weeks after he leaves, I know the ultimate purpose of this discussion is to come together as a group to help Baker and make sure his mind is in as good of a place as possible. No one can afford to be in a fog when they're out of the wire. Having a clear mind and the ability to make quick decisions can be the difference between life and death. I will say that the military takes care of their own.

After our meeting, Cooper and I opt to do a quick run before hitting the gym since we missed our morning one. When we're not out on missions, there isn't much to do on base besides work out, so we spend a lot of time in the gym.

It's a cool day with brisk winds that make it even colder. We run at a steady pace, neither of us feeling the need to push our bodies today.

"So, have you and London had Skype sex yet?" Cooper asks out of the blue.

"What?" I turn to him, my eyes wide, before facing forward again.

"You heard me."

"Um, no." I shake my head as we round the corner.

A group of Navy SEALs is running ahead of us.

Bagram is big, and the branches of the military are fairly segregated in that we each have a section of the base. Most of what we do here is with the Army, particularly our own unit, but we do cross-train with the Air Force and Navy on occasion.

I recognize the group of SEALs as the same one we trained with last week. We've been working out the logistics of a possible future mission. They're a great bunch of guys. If I were pushing myself today, I could pass them, and normally, I would love the competition, but I have no desire to do so today. This entire day has been emotionally and physically exhausting, and it's not even dinnertime yet.

"What are you waiting for? Maggie and I have done it, like, four times already."

"Really? Wow. I just…I don't know."

"Eh, it's your first tour with a girl back home. I get why you're a little slow to catch on. But I'm telling you, man, Skype sex is pretty great. You need to get on that shit, pronto."

I can't help the smile that crosses my face at Cooper's complete lack of conversational boundaries. He's never had them. From the moment he introduced himself to me and started talking back in basic training, he's been the same way.

"Hell yeah. I'm on it," I agree.

I can't believe I didn't think of it before. This deployment and all these feelings and shit have really been messing with my head.

All at once, several things happen. The familiar cracking of an M4 sounds in the distance. Panicked yelling comes from the group of men running ahead of us. I quickly take stock of my surroundings as the bullets continue to hit the ground, sending dirt particles flinging into the air.

"Holy shit!" I yell out.

Cooper and I duck behind a light pole. It doesn't provide much cover, but the illusion of cover allows my mind to process what's happening. I look to where the shots are coming from—the nearest guard tower.

Motherfucker.

It's an ANA—Afghan National Army—fucker. Part of our job over here is to train the ANA and ANP—Afghan National Police—to defend themselves against the Taliban. It's not uncommon to work with a group of Afghan dudes for months, just to have one of them, who is a supposed friend, turn. Many of our guys have been gunned down by a "friendly" Afghan who was really working for the other side.

Truthfully, it's one of the most difficult aspects of being here. We're trying to teach people to defend themselves, yet half of the time, they don't even care. We're losing guys to help people who don't even want us here. *What's the fucking point?*

The ANA helps us man our guard towers, and apparently, the one who is currently shooting at us has had an ulterior motive behind his act of wanting to keep the men within the wire safe.

Now, more guns join the chaos as the crack of the bullets come from other directions. Our guys are fighting back. The bullets stop hitting the dirt around us.

Cooper and I take the opportunity to run toward the group of Navy SEALs. In a matter of seconds, we're beside them. Two men are lying on the ground. I immediately recognize them—Ramirez and Johnson.

Red stains saturate their T-shirts as their brothers kneel beside them, working hastily to provide first aid.

"Let's get them to medical!" I shout.

Instantly, precision amid the chaos ensues as all the able-bodied men work as a unit to transport the injured to the medical building, which stands several city blocks away.

We run as smoothly as possible with the injured. Some of us help carry the men while a few run beside, applying pressure to the men's gushing wounds.

Once the men are laid on gurneys, the medical staff takes over, wheeling them into surgery.

The door to the base hospital shuts, and Cooper and I stand, facing it. Sweat drips from our faces, our chests heave from exhaustion, and blood from the wounded men begins to dry on our skin.

"What a fucked up day," Cooper grunts out as he raises his arms, entwining his hands around the back of his neck.

I let out a sigh in response.

A medic comes out to ask us all a few questions, and we give our verbal report of the event. Then, we head back to our section of base to shower.

"Do you think they'll make it?" Cooper asks.

"I don't know." I shake my head. "I think Ramirez was already gone." I loathe the words exiting my mouth.

"Johnson was still breathing, but he didn't look good." Cooper bows his head with a sigh.

"Fuckers," I growl, thinking about the Afghan soldiers whom I've been helping to train. I wonder if it was someone I knew. I hope it wasn't because I would hate myself for not being able to see the signs of his dishonesty.

"We should just leave this shithole," Cooper states, rage lining his voice. "They obviously don't want us here."

"I know." I nod, understanding his anger.

It's hard to risk your life and to see your brothers lose their lives for a cause that's often hard to find. I have to make myself remember the kind people I've met from the villages—men, women, and children—who don't want to be any part of the Taliban and the hatred they breed.

The Afghan people in general are very simple. The people in these villages live in another time. It's like stepping into the 1910s. Most have no electricity in their dirt-floor huts. They are hard workers, growing the plants and raising the animals that they eat. There's an innocence about them that makes me want to help them. I have to remind myself daily that they aren't the enemy but the victims in all of this.

I also have to remind myself that if we're over here, fighting with the enemy, then the enemy isn't back home, bombing innocent people. Their focus will be on us—the trained military. It's hard to be here. It's isolating at times, but I have to keep in mind why we're here, especially when the *why* is so difficult to comprehend.

After getting cleaned up, Cooper and I walk silently to the chow hall. We received news that neither soldier who was shot made it. It's definitely the worst day we've had since being here.

"A brilliant end to a shitastic day," I mumble before choking down a piece of lobster.

"It's like chewing fucking leather," Cooper complains between bites.

"Only forty-nine weeks to go!" I say with mock excitement, waving my fork in front of me.

"Is that all?" Cooper questions with thick sarcasm.

"Whatever dining contractor is working right now needs to be fired. The food's been shitty all week," Smith, a Special Forces brother from our unit, offers from across the table.

He's a cool guy, quiet for the most part. He lives with his wife in Perrysburg, Ohio.

"Yeah, it has!" Cooper agrees.

"Meat shouldn't be slimy," Smith mumbles, stabbing his fork into his lobster.

"Exactly! The breakfast sausage from yesterday slipped down my throat, like it was competing with the German luge team in the Winter Olympics, before I could even think about chewing the fucker."

A grumble of laughter sounds from the table.

"Well, did it earn a medal?" I ask with a smirk.

"Obviously, you know the Germans and Russians always medal in that event." Cooper smiles.

Cooper and I have a slight addiction to the Olympics. We watch almost every event the two weeks that it's on.

"How's Bethany?" I ask Smith, veering the subject away from slippery breakfast meats.

"She's great." His face lights up. "Did I tell you that she found out she was pregnant?"

"No," Cooper and I answer in unison.

Cooper says, "You all were having trouble in that department, right?"

"Yeah, we'd been trying for a couple of years. Go figure it happens right before I leave."

"That's pretty awesome, man. Congrats," I say. "Will you be able to get home for the birth?"

"Yeah, I'm hoping to catch it. I'm going to plan my mid tour around her due date. So, as long as she doesn't go real early or late, it should be good."

"That's sweet, man. Congrats again," Cooper says.

Mid tour is a two-week break that we get if we're deployed for a year or more. I've never taken one before because I've never had anyone to go home to. I haven't planned it yet or even told London about it out of fear that something would come up, mission-wise, and it wouldn't work out. I don't want to get her hopes up. But I'm really hoping that my schedule permits it this time around.

Back in my room after dinner, I'm thrilled when I see that London is online, and I Skype her.

"Oh my gosh!" Her beautiful face fills my laptop screen as she claps with excitement. "How are you? It's so good to see you! Wow...you're growing a beard. Ooh...you're totally hot with facial hair. What are you up to? How's Cooper? Are you staying safe? Tell me everything."

This, right here, London's beautiful innocence, is exactly what I needed after a day like today. After waking up to a bombing, almost getting shot on a run, watching someone die as I carried his bloody body to the hospital, and the nail in the coffin with the shitty food, this will definitely be going down as one of the worst days in my life. But looking at London's big brown eyes that haven't seen the cruelty in the world and her gorgeous smile that radiates naivety and love somehow makes it all better. She makes the horrible circumstances surrounding today bearable.

God, I love her.

"You asked so many questions that I forgot them all," I kid.

"I'm sorry. I'm just so freaking excited to see you!" She grins wide. "How are you? Are you okay?" Worry clouds her cheerful demeanor.

"Yeah, I'm great," I lie.

I know that London wants to have a one hundred percent honesty thing going on while I'm here. But that's actually a horrible idea. The obvious reason is that I can't tell her much of what happens here anyway, especially if it's mission-related. Plus, I don't see the value in telling her all the horrible stuff when there is nothing she can do to make it better, which, in turn, would upset her.

"Are you sure?" Her face tilts, as if she's studying me on her computer screen, her eyes squinting in question.

"Yeah." I force my smile to go wider. "Honestly, babe…I'm just a little tired, is all."

She nods. "I can see that. You look tired. I'm sorry."

"It's fine. I'll be heading to bed here shortly. No worries. Tell me, how are you?"

"Great. I'm heading to the airport in an hour. Georgia and I are flying into Kentucky to spend Christmas with our parents."

That's right. It's Christmas Eve. I forgot, yet the second I woke up this morning, I remembered that it was steak and lobster day.

"That's great. How long will you be there?"

"I'll be back in Michigan on the twenty-ninth, so not that long. I wanted to return in time to do something with Paige for New Year's. Actually, we're thinking about flying somewhere. Probably somewhere in Cali, so Georgia can join us. This is her first New Year's being twenty-one, so she can get into a real club. Anyway, I'm bringing my laptop to my parents', of course, so we'll be able to chat. We need to plan a time to Skype tomorrow. It is Christmas and all. Do you know your schedule?"

I think about my agenda for the next day. I'll be free after dinner, so that's about seven in the evening, which would be ten thirty in the morning for London. "I'm free anytime after ten thirty in the morning, your time."

"All right. We'll probably just be finishing opening presents then. So, how's noon, my time? Will you still be up?"

"Yeah, that works."

"Great. That will be in between presents and our early Christmas dinner. Everyone kind of does their own thing then, so I can head to my bedroom and give you my complete attention." London smiles wide.

"Do you have your own bedroom there?"

"Of course. Why do you ask?" London tilts her head to the side, an adorable smile lighting up her face.

"Well, I was talking to Cooper today—"

London cuts me off before I finish my thought, "Interesting because I was talking to Maggie yesterday." She puckers her lips together.

"Oh, yeah?" I chuckle. "And?"

"She was telling me about a certain Skype activity that she and Cooper do that we have not yet tried."

"Huh. You know, that's kind of a coincidence because Cooper was telling me about a Skype activity as well."

"So, you want to do it tomorrow?" She quirks up an eyebrow and bites her bottom lip.

"It would be a great Christmas present," I say playfully. "Will that be weird? In your parents' house?"

"No, believe me, it will be fine. First, my room is on the opposite side of the house of the main living area where everyone will be. Plus, I have a lock. No one will know. It's a huge house. Seriously, it will be totally great.

No worries." She claps her hands together before yelling, "Oh my God…I'm so excited!"

"You're so beautiful," I say with a laugh.

"You know, I'd rather actually be with you on our first Christmas. But, since we can't, Skype sex is the next best thing. Have you ever done it before?"

"No." I shake my head.

"Me neither. Another first for us."

"That, it is."

"So, what have you been up to? Any exciting plans for Christmas?"

Her deep brown eyes fringed in long black lashes threaten to steal my breath from over six thousand miles away.

I can't get over how much I love her. I never knew this love, these feelings, were possible. It's both terrifying and amazing at the same time.

Love…

It's so strange, surreal, and completely undeniable.

I blink hard, breaking the fog of adoration that had me momentarily paralyzed. "Um, not much. It's a typical day here. I'm sure the dining hall will serve something 'special'"—I use air quotes around the last word because *special* is subjective—"for dinner, probably roast beef or something. A change in the food menu is about as much celebration as we get here on base."

"Are there any bars or anything around, so you can go out and celebrate?"

I shake my head. "No. Actually, there are two general orders on base that must be followed. Number one is, no sex in the AOR, which means Area of Responsibility. So, that's like the entire base. Number two is, no alcohol. I don't think the guys in charge think it's a good idea to have drunk dudes walking around with firearms, you know?"

London nods in understanding. "Oh, yeah. Two very good rules. Not that either applies to you." She winks.

Man, I wish she weren't about to leave for the airport because a bout of Skype sex sounds incredible right about now. Seeing her face makes me miss her even more.

"Exactly. You're not here, and I don't drink anyway." I take a moment just to gaze into the screen to take her in. "You know, I'll probably just go to the gym, hang with Cooper, watch a movie with some of the guys, maybe play some cards, but none of that compares to what I'll be doing at eight thirty in the evening." I stare intently.

She squeals excitedly. "Oh, I love you."

She leans in and presses her lips in front of her laptop's camera, so all I can see on my end are her plump lips taking up my screen.

"Muah!" she says before blowing me a virtual kiss. "I've gotta go, babe, so I don't miss my flight. I still have to finish packing before I leave." Disappoint sounds in her voice.

"That's okay. I'm just so happy that I was able to catch you online. Plus, I'll see you tomorrow, right?"

"Right!"

"All right. Bye, baby. Have a safe flight."

"I will. You stay safe. I will see you tomorrow."

She blows another kiss toward the camera before she clicks out of Skype, and I'm left staring at a blank screen.

Well, it was a shitastic day, but at least it ended on a good note. I let the vision of London fill my head as I lie back on my pillow.

Maybe tonight, for once, I can dream of her, of happiness. Though something tells me that's not going to happen.

FIFTEEN

London

"There's just something unnatural and depressing about celebrating a special occasion without the one you love."
—*London Wright*

"Merry Christmas, baby," Loïc's gorgeous face says from the computer screen.

"Merry Christmas," I respond as a blanket of happiness falls over me.

I said good-bye to Loïc twenty-one days ago, and that time has been, without a doubt, the longest twenty-one days of my life. Yet all of that longing dissipates, or at least lessens, when I get to see his living, breathing, smiling face—even if it is on a screen.

I couldn't wait to see him today. I miss Loïc all the time, but the ache is fiercer when it's a holiday. There's just something unnatural and depressing about celebrating a special occasion without the one you love.

"How was your day?" I ask. "Do anything special?"

"Well, we had roast beef in the chow hall, which was a treat for the holiday." Loïc shrugs.

"Was it good?" I ask with a laugh.

"It was edible. Cooper would tell you different though."

"That's because Cooper is a fantastic chef and knows how food should be."

"True. He has less patience for the crap they call food over here." Loïc pauses to think before continuing, "Some of the guys threw around some tinsel and green and red garland in the rec building."

"That's festive."

"Yeah, I suppose it is. But, more than anything, it's a pain in the ass. That silver tinsel shit sticks to everything. We've all been walking around base today with shreds of silver hanging on us."

I grin at the vision of all the guys in their camouflage fatigues and the tinsel blowing in a cheerful dance from their bodies.

Loïc's expression goes serious before he says, "I miss you, babe."

I let out a sigh. "I miss you, too."

"So, your day is going well?"

"Yeah, we opened presents this morning and had a big breakfast. Now, we're all relaxing before dinner."

"Sounds good."

"It'd be better if you were here, but, yeah…it's good." I steer this conversation away from depressing to exciting as I cut to the chase, "So, are we ready to exchange presents?" I pucker my lips in a grin, raising an eyebrow.

"Oh, I'm ready." Loïc smiles big.

"How do we do this exactly?" I ask, suddenly feeling a little shy and awkward.

"How about you start by removing your clothes?" Loïc's voice changes. It's deeper, huskier, and it sends a chill down my spine as I realize we're officially doing this.

I comply with his command and watch as he removes his as well.

"Turn around—slowly," he says. "I want to take you all in."

I do as he asked until I'm facing my laptop screen again.

"Grab your nipples for me, babe," Loïc says in a raspy voice. "Tug on them a little."

I do as instructed while closing my eyes and pretending Loïc's hands are on me.

"That's it," he coaxes.

I open my eyes to see his dilated blues intently watching me. His arm is moving slowly back and forth, but the camera cuts off right below his elbow.

"Move back, so I can see you," I breathe out. Any apprehension that I had is gone, replaced by nothing but raw lust.

He sits further away from his laptop, and my entire body starts to vibrate with sexual energy as I watch Loïc touching himself. I'm surprised at how much it turns me on.

I exhale as one of my hands leaves my boob to travel south. My fingers enter my body as my other hand continues to tug at my nipple. I think of Loïc and the magic that his fingers are capable of yielding, and I mimic his past movements. The pleasure is incredible, and I let out a moan, my head falling back.

"Yes, baby…that's it," Loïc says. "That's great, baby. Just like that."

Hearing him fuels my desire, and I begin to ride my fingers, desperate to feel Loïc inside me.

Loïc and I are close to perfect for each other in all aspects, but our compatibility in the bedroom is out of this world. I pull out all the memories of us—moans, pleasure, kisses…his lips, hands, and mouth. I love it rough and soft, anyway I can get it, because it's incredible with him, every time. In one movement, Loïc's body can fill me up, pushing everything out, until I can't focus on anything but the sensations he gives me.

"Loïc," I cry, my entire body humming.

"I'm here," he breathes harshly.

And he is. I can feel his mouth on me as his hands tug with the precise amount of pressure on my nipples. He's inside me, and it's perfection, as always.

God, I love him. I need him. I'm his forever, and he's mine.

That last thought sends me over the edge, and I crumble. My entire core pulses with bliss, and my body quivers in release. I let go of everything plaguing me—the worry, the longing, and the sadness. Instead, my body fills with intense satisfaction and immense feelings of love, loyalty, and visions of forever. My heart overflows with adoration, and I call out Loïc's name. It's the only name I want to associate with these feelings for the rest of my life.

I've found my nirvana, and his name is Loïc Berkeley.

I open my eyes in time to see Loïc groan in release. His head falls back against the chair as his fist pumps hard, producing evidence of his pleasure.

It's the single hottest thing I've ever seen in my life, and I can't help but stare in amazement. His muscles are tight with a shimmer of sweat as his stroke slows, and I can't help but think that he looks like a Greek god, my freaking Adonis. He's so perfect, and he doesn't even know it.

He lifts his head, and his eyes open to find mine.

We stare in silence. It's easy to know the thoughts going through his mind because they're the same ones going through mine.

Finally, I break the silence by saying, "We are definitely doing that more often."

He throws his head back again but this time in laughter.

His body moves from the camera as he grabs a towel. I do the same. After I clean up, I put my clothes back on to find Loïc dressed and waiting on my laptop screen.

"So…how was it for you?" He smirks.

"Surprisingly amazing," I answer. "You know, I thought it was going to be a little awkward, but honestly, it wasn't at all. I just imagined you and I together. It wasn't as good as having you here with me, but it was a close second. How was it for you?"

"Bloody brilliant!" he exclaims with a goofy grin.

I laugh.

"English-accent worthy, huh?"

"Fuck yeah, baby. That's as good as it gets over here. You're right, we're absolutely going to be finding time to do that more often." His face goes serious before he asks, "What did I do to deserve you?"

"You were yourself, and you, Loïc, my love, are pretty incredible."

On instinct, I reach my fingers out to touch the screen. His hand rises until his fingers are touching his screen almost seven thousand miles away. It's not the same, not even close. But, if I concentrate hard enough, I can almost feel him, the real him, and it's the most fantastic sensation in the world.

SIXTEEN

London

"If Loïc were anyone other than who he is, I would be hooking up with the Calvin Klein model in front of me at this very moment and writing my Dear Loïc letter in the morning."
—London Wright

I understand why Dear John letters are so common. I truly do. The fact of the matter is that long-distance relationships suck.

Like, really blow.

If Loïc were anyone other than who he is, I would be hooking up with the Calvin Klein model in front of me at this very moment and writing my Dear Loïc letter in the morning. Loïc would be nothing more than some fond memories, tinged with a splash of regret.

But, lucky for the both of us, he's not someone I can replace. He's a once-in-a-lifetime love that I know I will never find again if I let him go.

So, instead, I swing back my hand and let my open palm strike the gorgeous man across his cheek. His hand flies to his face where he rubs the spot I just hit.

"What the fuck?" he yells at me with anger as his eyes bulge.

"I told you that I didn't want to dance," I state the obvious, shrugging my shoulders, as if smacking hot men in clubs is something I do on a regular basis.

"And that gives you the right to fucking hit me?" he screeches in rage, his voice rising more than one octave.

"Your hand on my ass sure does. Chances are, if I don't want to dance with you, I surely don't want you groping my ass."

He inhales, his chest expands, as if he's about to let a slur of obscenities fly my way, before he blows the air out in a huff and stomps away from me.

I'm about ninety-nine percent sure though that I hear him say, "Bitch," as he goes.

"Londy, he was so cute," Georgia whines beside me, pouting out her lips.

"Yeah, but I have Loïc."

"So? I don't. You could have at least directed him toward Paige or me before you assaulted his beautiful face. Did you see those dimples?"

"Oh, I saw them," Paige says with a sigh. "And the eyes."

"And the jaw," Georgia says dreamily.

"And the tan skin. His chest looked rock hard." Paige stares off into the sea of dancing bodies, as if she's dying to get another look at him.

"And his ass. Did you see his ass, Paige?" Georgia says with a slight shriek.

I raise my hands in surrender. "I'm sorry. I wasn't thinking," I say with a laugh.

"You clearly weren't," Georgia agrees.

"I was just trying to be a good girlfriend."

"You accomplished that. But you weren't a good wingwoman. Not. At. All," Georgia complains with a roll of her eyes.

"You know what they say, London. *Curiosity killed the cat*." Paige shrugs.

"No, it didn't," I deadpan.

"You put us between a rock and a hard place?" Paige questions, her eyebrow quirking up.

"No." I shake my head, straight-faced.

"How about, you could've killed two birds with one stone?" Georgia chimes in.

"Yes," I point toward Georgia while addressing Paige, "that's the one. That saying makes actual sense."

"I suppose," Paige says with a shrug of her shoulders.

"So, we're agreed. If that happens again, then you will very politely shut him down while effectively directing him our way?" Georgia asks.

"Yes, okay. I get it," I say with an air of annoyance. "Let's go get another drink."

"Well, McHottie could have been buying us drinks as we speak," Paige says under her breath in a resigned tone.

"Oh my God, let it go already! Plus, we can buy our own damn drinks." I say before turning to beeline it to the bar.

I wish Loïc were here.

Loïc's presence would solve all my problems. I wouldn't have to smack guys, get in arguments with Paige and Georgia, or feel sad because I have no one to kiss at midnight.

After getting our cosmos, we stand in front of the bar and sip them.

"See that guy over there in the tight black T-shirt?" Georgia motions toward a group of guys standing to the right of the main dance floor.

"Which one?" I see that four out of the group of six are wearing black shirts.

"The one closest to us with the black hair," she answers.

"Yeah."

"Well, he's the one I'm going to be kissing in"—she pulls her cell phone out of her wristlet and looks to the screen—"one hour and forty-four minutes."

"Good choice," Paige agrees.

"Who are you going after?" I ask Paige.

"Um, I don't know." She mindlessly scans the club.

"You can hug me at midnight! Who needs boys?" I wrap my free hand around Paige's waist.

"We do!" Georgia answers. "Just because you're all committed for life at twenty-two doesn't mean we have to be lame along with you. Right, Paige?"

"Right! I want to make out with a cute boy! It's New Year's!" Paige answers.

"Hey, I'm almost twenty-three." My statement is met with silence, as if this little fact doesn't mean anything to them, which I suppose it doesn't. "Yeah, and nothing says, *Happy New Year*, like sticking your tongue in a stranger's mouth," I argue. Dropping my hand from Paige's side, I pick up the lemon slice from the rim of my glass and suck on it. My face automatically scrunches up from the tartness.

Georgia waves me off. "Ignore her. She's just jealous. Come on, Paige. My guy has five hot friends for you to pick from."

The two of them are off before I have a chance to argue my case any further. But, honestly, I'm just being selfish. Just because I have to spend my evening alone doesn't mean they have to. Georgia's right. I am jealous.

Ever since I've been going to New Year's parties, my first one at the age of sixteen, I've always kissed someone at midnight. Hell, I don't even remember who I kissed most of those years, but it was someone.

This year, I actually have someone I'm in love with, and I'm spending the holiday alone. It sucks. If Loïc were any of my previous boyfriends, I wouldn't have hesitated to use the I-was-drunk excuse when I explained to him the next day that I'd kissed someone else and I now had to break up. But everything is different now that I'm with Loïc. I've changed. It's good.

I follow Paige and Georgia toward the group of guys. *What else am I going to do? Stand by myself?*

Georgia is already working her magic on Black Shirt Number One. Honestly though, she doesn't ever have to work too hard. Paige is chatting with another guy in the group as well.

"Why the frown?"

It takes me a second longer than it should to realize that the cute guy is talking to me.

I quickly take him in. He's freaking Brad Pitt from *Legends of the Fall* but with short hair.

What's up with the people of LA? Are they all freaking models?

And he's wearing a white shirt. I love a guy who stands out from the crowd.

"I'm sorry?" I question for lack of anything better to say. I might be taken, but I still have eyes and hormones. I'd be lying if I said my body wasn't reacting to the dude.

"You don't look too happy, standing here. Everything okay?"

And he's sensitive and sweet. *Of course he is.*

"I'm fine. Just thinking." I smile.

"I'm Brad," he says, holding out his hand.

"You've got to be kidding me." I laugh. Shaking his hand, I say, "London," through a chuckle.

He turns his head to the side. "Didn't realize my name was so comical."

"Sorry, inside joke. Just something I was thinking. It's not you."

He seems to accept my explanation. "London's a cool name."

"Thanks."

"So—" he begins.

But I cut him off, "Look, Brad, I'm sure you're a nice guy, but I'm not interested."

He appears momentarily shocked before recovering. "Not interested in talking to me?"

"Talking or basically anything else. I have a boyfriend," I say by way of explanation.

"Okay? So, you can't speak to people if you have a boyfriend?"

"Well, you know how it is. No one in these places is here to make friends. It's just better to be up-front. Sorry if I'm coming off as rude, but I just don't want to deal with it."

"Deal with a decent guy talking to you because you were standing here, looking sad?"

"Yeah," I say bluntly.

I've come to realize that I'm kind of a bitch, and I've accepted this fact.

Brad does the last thing that I expected him to do. He laughs, like all-out, head-thrown-back laughter.

When he faces me again, he says, "You're hilarious."

"Um, thanks?" I peer up to his bright blue eyes.

"Listen, London, I'm not interested in hooking up with you or anything else that would come in between you and your boyfriend."

"You're not?" I tilt my head to the side, examining the sincerity in his features.

"No, I was just trying to be nice."

"Oh," I answer sheepishly.

"Last time I checked, talking isn't cheating."

"It's not."

"Okay then." He smirks. "Do you live in LA?"

He's right. There's no harm in talking to someone. It beats standing here, brooding in my own misery.

"No, Michigan actually. My sister lives in Palo Alto. She's in her senior year at Stanford." I motion toward Georgia, who has her hands on Black Shirt's chest.

"Ah, I see."

"Do you live in LA?"

"Yeah, I live in the Hill Section of Manhattan Beach."

"Oh, nice," I attempt to say nonchalantly though I've been to one of my dad's business associate's homes in that neighborhood and know how upscale it is. *Cute and rich? Totally not fair.*

"So, London, what do you do in Michigan?"

"Well, I'm a journalist. I write freelance articles for a local online news outlet, but I'm looking for another job."

"Oh, yeah? Why's that?"

"I love my job—don't get me wrong—but I need more. I'm a little bored. I'm applying to bigger newspapers and news stations. In my line of employment, you have to work your way up from the bottom, you know? I mean, I'm sure I could have used some of father's connections to get a better first job, but I liked starting out small. I've learned a lot. Now, I'm ready to learn more."

"That's great."

"Yeah. So, what do you do out here?"

"Well, I'm a senior editor for the *Los Angeles Times*."

My mouth falls open in what I'm sure is a very unattractive way before I snap it shut. "You are not!"

"I am." He smiles.

"How old are you?" I question.

He doesn't look old enough to be a senior of anything.

"Twenty-eight."

"Huh," I let out.

"Yeah, too bad you don't live out this way. I might have a job for you." He winks, grinning wide.

I'm momentarily stunned at just how attractive he is.

"No way!" I shriek as I grab his arm.

Wait, I can't live out here.

I release my grasp. "Well, I have to stay in Michigan." I sigh.

"The boyfriend?"

"Yeah."

"If you don't mind me asking, why isn't he here?"

"He's in the military. He's overseas in Afghanistan right now."

"Ah," he makes a sound of understanding. "That must be hard."

"It is," I agree.

"You have to drill me!" I exclaim louder than necessary.

"I'm sorry?"

"Drill me with questions. Like, if I were in an interview with the paper, what would you ask me? I might not be able to work at your paper, but you could help me with what to say in my interviews with others. You know, show me what you people are looking for."

"Us people?" He chuckles. "Okay, let's order some drinks and talk shop, shall we?"

"Yes, let's!"

"All right, we have a table reserved over there." He points to a table in the corner of the VIP section. It's surrounded by a semicircular cushioned bench.

I tell Paige and Georgia where I am going to be. Each girl seems interested in their make-out buddy of choice for the evening and barely care that I'm stepping away. I follow Brad to his table, and a waitress comes to take our order.

"Can we have a bottle of Dom Perignon Rose?" he asks the server.

She smiles politely before leaving the table.

"You didn't need to order that," I say, knowing that the particular bottle of champagne usually costs around four hundred dollars in a place like this.

"You don't like champagne?"

"No, I do. But I would have been fine with a glass of something else." *Less expensive*, I think to myself.

"It's fine. We need to celebrate."

"We do?" I question.

"Of course. We need to toast to the New Year, for one. And to new friends."

I have to stop myself from saying the rude comment hovering on the tip of my tongue about how he's awfully presumptuous to assume that I want to be his friend. After all, he does seem like a sincerely nice guy who just wants to talk. And I could learn a lot from him. I suppose if I can't make out with Loïc at midnight, the next best thing is to talk to Brad and get tips on how to advance my career.

The champagne comes, and Brad keeps filling my glass. I'm so glad he ordered it. It's so delicious. He really did help turn this horrible night into a positive one.

Brad's so smart. I don't think I've ever had such an enjoyable and informative conversation with someone about my line of work before. We talk about everything from what I should put on my résumé to how I should answer interview questions to the types of pieces that the paper loves to print and the experience they like to see in the journalists they hire.

My head is starting to feel a little fuzzy, so to make sure that I won't forget any information Brad is telling me, I type it all out in my Notes app on my phone.

"Let me see what you've put." He reaches out for my phone, and I give it to him.

He starts typing something.

"What are you doing?" I ask.

"You forgot a few key pieces of information," he answers but doesn't look up from the phone.

After a minute, he hands it back to me, and I look down to what he typed. His name, Brad Abernathy, is spelled out, followed by a cell phone number, a work number, an email address, and an address.

"Why did you give me your address?" I peer up from my phone to find his bold blue eyes focused on me.

He seems closer, our faces only a foot apart.

"In case you ever need it."

"Why would I need it?" My stare darts from his eyes to his lips before I close my eyes tight and drop my face toward my lap, trying to center myself.

His warm fingers press against the bottom of my chin, lifting my face up until our eyes meet again. "London, call me anytime if you have any more questions. Feel free to use me as a reference on your résumé. Whatever you need, okay?"

"Okay, thank you," I whisper, still thrown off-balance with his slight touch.

I raise my hands to grab his and pull it down away from my face. His free hand covers both of mine, and we're a jumbled pile of hands in his lap. I try to pull away, but he holds my hands tightly in his grasp.

"London?" he asks quietly, his voice low and raspy.

"Yeah?"

"Your boyfriend's a lucky guy."

I swallow the lump in my throat that seems to be stuck, and I'm finding it hard to breathe.

"London?" he asks again, this time rubbing his thumb across the skin of my hand.

"Yeah?"

"Happy New Year," he says before closing his eyes and leaning in toward me.

Suddenly, my hazy mind is sharp. My surroundings, which were previously muted, are coming in crystal clear.

The confetti.

The music.

The celebration.

Brad's lips, so close to mine.

I shake the remainder of fog from my brain before shouting, "No!"

I scoot back across the bench before Brad's lips can touch mine. In a beat, I've distanced myself from Brad, like he's a fire about to engulf me in its flames. And, in a way, he is.

I will not succumb to the flames because I know I will be left with nothing but smoldering ashes.

"I've gotta go!" I cry, panicked.

I feel his fingers close around my wrist, and I vaguely register his pleading words of apology, but I shake him off me and exit the booth. I spot Georgia and Paige right away. Both of them are standing to the side of the dance floor where I left them earlier, lip-locked with Black Shirt One and Two.

I don't want to ruin their evening, but I have to get out of here. I jog toward the exit as best I can in my heels and enter a waiting taxi.

On the short drive to the hotel, I text both Paige and Georgia, letting them know that I'm all right but that I headed back to the room early. I caution them to stick together and be careful before telling them to have fun.

Back in the room, I start up my laptop, which I take everywhere with me so that I can connect with Loïc every day in some way or another.

I pray that he's online. I look to the time. It's just before twelve thirty LA time, so it'd be almost noon his time. *Maybe he has a break after lunch, and he's on his laptop?*

I begin to cry when the little circle next to his name doesn't pop up green. He's not online, and there's something so devastating about that because I need to see his face now more than ever.

My tears fall harder. Bending my face to my hands, I sob. My body shudders with sadness as my tears continue to fall.

As I cry, I try to make sense of the last hour and a half. I feel so incredibly guilty. Yes, I found Brad attractive, but I didn't want to do anything with him. I truly didn't. I never want to hurt Loïc, and I can't think of anything that would hurt him more than me cheating on him.

I didn't kiss Brad, but he almost kissed me. *Is that my fault? Was I sending out the wrong signals? Was it wrong of me to get work advice?*

So many questions are bouncing around within my skull, and I can't think clearly enough to answer any of them.

All I know is that I love Loïc. I want Loïc, and I don't want anyone else. Not now, not ever. I don't care if Brad does look like a hot actor and he has my dream job. I don't want him.

Maybe it's a blessing that Loïc isn't online to see me like this. It would just upset him and make him worry.

Opening my email, I find a new one from him. At least I have that.

When I attempt to read it though, I get nauseous, and the room starts to spin. Too much champagne, too many emotions, and not enough Loïc make for a shitty night.

I drink a huge glass of water before plopping into bed. Maybe I'll get to chat with Loïc in the morning. Until then, I'm going to dream about my beautiful warrior. He's the only one for me.

I know, without a doubt, that he's the only one I want.

Just Loïc.
Just Loïc.
Just Loïc.

To: Loïc Berkeley

From: London Wright

Subject: Question 27

Hello. I hope everything is going great and that you're staying safe. Not much going on here. I'm just spending the day writing some articles, and Paige is working late.

To answer your latest question, my favorite cereal is Fruity Pebbles.

Question 27: What's your favorite number? Mine's sixteen. I'm not sure why. I've just always liked it.

I love you. Stay safe.

Love,

London

I read the email over, debating on whether or not to add more to it, but I don't know what else to put. Sighing, I hit Send. It will have to do. I'll do better on my email tomorrow.

I've been in such a funk since New Year's, and I'm not sure why. I know I didn't do anything wrong where Brad was concerned. *Or maybe I did unknowingly?* I'm not sure, but my intentions were in the right place.

Perhaps my sour mood has nothing to do with Brad and everything to do with the fact that I just miss Loïc.

I knew this long-distance-relationship deal would be hard, but, man, it sucks.

Loïc seems to think we will be able to find a time to Skype in the next few days, which is great. I need to see him.

Yeah, everything will be better when I can see him.

SEVENTEEN

Loïc
Age Eight
New Hope, Mississippi

"It's so hard to be brave when I'm so scared. But I have to be."
—Loïc Berkeley

I walk into the side kitchen door to find my mom frosting my birthday cake.

"How was your day, Loïc, love?" she says with a wide smile.

I answer her with a big hug as I wrap my arms around her waist. I love when Mom is happy.

Dad bursts into the kitchen. "I thought I heard a birthday boy in here. Come on, come on," he says to Mom and me. He grabs our hands and leads out the door and to the backyard.

I stand in the center of the square of grass that makes up our yard and expectantly look around.

"I spy with my little eye something that is red," my dad says, his eyes shining with happiness.

I turn in a circle in the middle of the small grassy space, but I can't find anything that's red.

"I spy two wheels…twenty-inch wheels," he clarifies.

I gasp and frantically search.

"With six speeds," he adds.

"Where is it? Where is it, Dad?" I shout, feeling so happy.

He nods toward the garage, and I take off running until I'm in the building, standing in front of the coolest bike ever—an awesome, shiny red six-speed mountain bike. It's like the one that boy down the street has, except way cooler.

"Thank you!" I shout as I jump into my dad's arms.

He lets me down, and I hug my mom.

"Thank you so much! I love it!"

I can't believe they got me the bike. I really wanted it, but I thought it was too expensive. I glance over to the worn green bike leaning against the wall of the garage. It's the bike I've had since I was four. Even though it hasn't had its training wheels for a long time, it still looks like a baby bike to me. Dad had raised the seat all the way up, but I could barely ride it because it was too small. But, now, I have a big-boy bike, a real bike.

"Happy birthday, Loïc," my dad says as he pulls me into another big hug.

The memory of my seventh birthday plays in my mind. I can't believe it was one year ago already.

I wish it were still my seventh birthday. Actually, I wish my parents were here to celebrate my eighth birthday with me.

I twirl the Happy Birthday pencil that I got from my new teacher between my fingers. If it weren't for school, I probably wouldn't have even known it was my birthday. Dwight and Stacey haven't said anything about it. I'm sure they won't.

My mom and dad used to tape streamers and balloons onto the outside frame of my door, so when I woke up on my birthday, I would have to break through them to get out. I loved that.

I loved everything.

I haven't even been here for a whole month yet, but it's been the worst few weeks of my life. I'm trying to be strong, but truthfully, I hate everything about this place. I hate the smell. I hate the dirt. I hate Dwight.

And, mostly, I hate that my mom and dad died.

I hate it! I hate it! I hate it!

I drop the pencil onto the dingy brown carpet and bury my face in my bent knees. *Why did this have to happen to me? It's not fair!* Silent tears soak the knees of my pants. I'm trying to be quiet so that they forget I'm here.

My back still stings from where Dwight threw me against the wall yesterday. I'm sure it's bruised, but I don't have a mirror to look.

My dad never hurt me. He never even spanked me. I don't even know why Dwight got so mad at me. I didn't do anything. I've been trying to be extra good, so he won't be angry. I don't understand it.

I can't figure out why I'm here and not in London with Nan and Granddad. I don't know who to ask either. When I asked Stacey if I could speak to my grandparents, she just laughed and said that no one was coming for me. It wasn't a happy laugh but a mean one. I hadn't realized until then that there was such a thing as a mean laugh. When my parents had laughed, their whole bodies would vibrate with happiness.

I miss happiness. It's nonexistent here. Of course, my world is covered in heartache, but even Dwight and Stacey seem to be miserable, like all the time.

Why do they even want a child?

I have so many questions and not a single answer. I just don't understand why any of this is happening. There are people in this world who love me. *So, why am I not with them? How do I get to them? How do I get out of here?*

My dad always told me that I was strong and brave, a warrior. That thought, as I'm crouched in a ball on my bedroom floor, makes me cry harder. It's so hard to be brave when I'm so scared. But I have to be.

I know that Nan and Granddad are looking for me, and when they find me, we'll be happy. When they find me, I won't have to be strong anymore because they'll take care of me. They'll love me and keep me safe. So, I just have to be brave for a little bit—until my grandparents come.

Maybe they'll be here tomorrow. I can be brave for one more day. I can do anything for one day.

I let my body fall to the side until my face is lying on the carpet. It has a yucky smell, but it's soft enough. My eyes close against the grimy brown material. I'm so tired, and my body's worn out from crying.

I feel myself drifting off to sleep, and I welcome it. I hope my dreams take me someplace happy. A small smile comes to my face as I look forward to tomorrow. I feel brave and strong.

Tomorrow, they'll come.

Tomorrow, I'll be happy again.

EIGHTEEN

Loïc

*"She's everything that I never had the courage to wish for,
but for some reason, I was lucky enough to find her.
Now that I've found her, I just hope I can keep her."*
—Loïc Berkeley

Damn it!

I bolt up to a sitting position and drag my fingers through my damp hair. I hate how long and unkempt it feels already. Absentmindedly, I drop one of my hands to my beard, which has a good half inch of growth already. In the Special Forces, we are encouraged to let our hair grow so that we'll blend in on our missions. But let's face it; there's no way in hell we are blending in here. Most of the guys love it. It's an excuse not to shave every day. It annoys me, but honestly, everything does, especially my damn nightmares that are back to being a nightly occurrence.

I've never been more ready for a deployment to be over, and I'm only a month in. There's this air of unease that follows me around like a suffocating fog. I keep searching, waiting for something to happen, for a ball to drop. It's exhausting, but I can't shake the feeling.

Maybe this is how all guys who leave behind someone they love feel. I've never had to deal with the paranoia before because I've never left anyone I've loved. I trust London. I do. I believe that what we have is real. Yet I'm constantly worried that she's going to leave me, cheat on me, get bored of waiting. Name it, and I've thought of it.

It's insane—these irrational thoughts. Yet, at the same time, I've watched guys' marriages fall apart while on deployment, and some of them had been married for years. It makes my seven-month relationship almost laughable. Regardless of the duration, it's the most meaningful relationship of my life, and I can't lose it.

I can't lose her.

London isn't just my end objective; she's the entire mission. She's my life from here on out. I never thought I would love someone the way I love her. I could never have imagined needing someone the way I need her. She's everything I never had the courage to wish for, but for some reason, I was lucky enough to find her. Now that I've found her, I just hope I can keep her.

So, add my fears of losing London to the place of hopelessness and loss that enshrouds me when I wake from a nightmare, and I'm a fucking basket case.

I'm so tired of dreaming of the scared boy, the pain, the loss, the fear of losing Sarah. I'm so sick of thinking about all of it. I want to move on to a place where I can be happy. London has shown me that true happiness is possible, and I want it—with her.

It's maddening that my brain won't cooperate. I just want to forget it all, except for her.

Is that too much to ask?

I quickly throw on my running gear and exit my room. I pound on the door next to mine until a tired Cooper answers.

"The fuck, dude?" he huffs out.

"You ready?"

His eyes drop to my feet before they make their way up to my face, as if his tired mind is trying to figure out what's going on. Some clarity lights his eyes. "Why are you up already? We weren't planning on going running for, like, another hour."

He looks back into his dark room, and I know he's looking at his alarm clock.

"Like an hour and a half actually," he grunts.

"Well, I couldn't sleep. You coming, or you want me to go without you?"

"I'm coming." He runs his hands through his longer hair, which is so thick that it almost stands up straight on its own. "Let me get dressed real quick," he says before letting the plywood door swing shut in my face.

A minute later, we're running through the dark base, the only light coming from the dim streetlights. Cooper doesn't say anything when I follow our ten-mile route even though today was supposed to be a six-mile run.

My feet pound against the ground, and I push my body until it screams in pain with each breath, but I don't stop. Running is the best stress reliever I have access to in this country, and I'm going to take advantage of it.

We don't talk the entire time, not that we could anyway.

When we reach the end of the run, Cooper bends at his waist and lets out a groan as his hands rest on his knees. His chest rises and falls as he tries to catch his breath. I put my hands behind my head, trying to stretch my lungs so that they can take in air more efficiently.

Finally, Cooper says, "Did you time us?"

I shake my head.

"Damn. I bet we beat our time, too."

"Probably," I agree.

"Bad night?" he questions.

"Something like that," I answer as we start walking toward our rooms.

After I shower, I power up my laptop, hoping to find London online, but I know that it's midnight, Michigan time, and a weekday, so she's probably sleeping.

Sure enough, she's not online at the moment. We've been able to Skype a few times since I've been here, and that's my favorite. It almost feels like we're not almost seven thousand miles away from each other.

I have a new email from her.

To: Loïc Berkeley

From: London Wright

Subject: Question 31

Hey, babe. It was so fun Skyping with you yesterday. We need to work out times when we can do that more often.

It's the best. I know you said that your schedule changes a lot and you don't know when you'll be around the computer, but still…we should try to set up some chat dates—at least when you know you'll be around.

Well, to answer question 30, if I had to live without one sense…I'd agree with you that it'd have to be smell. I couldn't live without seeing, hearing, or touching you. And I really love tasting my food. Although not being able to taste would be a hell of a diet plan—not that I follow a diet plan now, but you know what I mean. So, it'd be smell. Though there would definitely be some scents that I would miss incredibly, number one being the smell of your cologne or body wash or whatever it is that makes you smell so delicious. I'd also miss the smell of spring and the flowers and the smell of food…particularly freshly baked bread or cookies. The smell of those is almost as good as the taste.

Nothing new is really going on here since my last email. I'm still exhausted from my New Year's trip to LA with Georgia and Paige. I think I've told you already, but I really hope this is the last New Year's that we'll spend apart. I don't want to ever start another New Year without you by my side. In fact, all the stuff that we're missing as a couple—our birthdays, Christmas, Valentine's...all the holidays—I hope we never have to celebrate those apart again.

Although I will say that, hands down, our Skype sex on Christmas was the best gift I've ever received. Oh! That just gave me an idea...

Question 31: What's the best present you've ever gotten? I just told you mine. ;-)

I have to sign off and finish writing a few articles.

I love you, babe. I hope you're safe and happy. Talk to you soon.

Love,

London

I'm relieved after reading London's email. The tone of it is much more upbeat than it has been for the past few days. I'm so glad that I got to see her face on Skype yesterday. I think that's all she needed, too. On the days following New Year's, her emails weren't the same. I don't know how to explain it, but there was just something off about them. They were shorter than usual and lacking London's flair. Even though her words were positive enough, they felt sad, if that makes any sense. This long-distance relationship is no joke. I don't envy the guys who have had to leave girlfriends and wives for multiple tours.

I've just started typing my reply to London when Cooper walks in, freshly showered, and plops down on my bed.

"Seriously?" I twist in the chair to face him.

"Whatever. You're the one who interrupted my beauty sleep."

"So, what? Since we have some extra time now, you've come to annoy me?" I quirk up an eyebrow.

"Basically. Annoy you, talk to you? Same difference lately." He shrugs, eyeing me with mock annoyance.

I give him the one-second finger before I turn back to the laptop and quickly finish my email to London.

To: London Wright

From: Loïc Berkeley

Subject: Question 32

The answer to your question is so simple...it's you. You are the greatest gift in my life.

Question 32: If you could live anywhere in the world, where would you want to live? Before, I would have said Michigan. I love the four seasons and all the outside activities available to do in each season. But, now, I would say wherever you are because I'm a lovesick sap, and I miss you like crazy.

Miss you, baby.

I love you.

Love,

Loïc

I have an unanswered email from Sarah as well, but I decide to write her another time. I close the laptop and turn the chair so that it faces the bed.

"Sorry, man. I've just been so freaking edgy lately," I say in response to his comment about him annoying me.

"I get it. No need to apologize."

If anyone gets it, it's Cooper. He's put up with my shit more than anyone. He's seen me much moodier. I mean, this is the guy who had a weeklong one-sided conversation with me when we first met in basic training. *Who talks to someone for an entire week, just to be ignored?* I know, if the roles were reversed, I would have moved on after he'd ignored my first question…let alone a week of questions.

"How do you do it?" I ask seriously.

"What?"

"Leave Maggie, stay sane…you know, all of it."

"It is what it is, man. There's no sense in driving yourself crazy over it, you know?"

I let out a halfhearted chuckle. "Easier said than done. How do you not let it drive you crazy?"

"You just have to focus on what you have control over. You can't focus on all the stuff you wish you could do because you'll go insane. So, for example…I wish I could see Maggie today—hug her, kiss her, make love to her—"

"I get the picture," I scoff.

"But I can't, right? So, I try not to think about that. Instead, I think about what I can do. I can email her. I can reread the emails she's sent, look at pictures of her—you know, stuff like that. I also make a checklist in my mind of what I'm going to accomplish today. I've already checked off a kick-ass run. So, next on my agenda is trying something new for breakfast, learning something new at our brief today, stuff like that."

"Trying something new at breakfast?" I almost can't get the question out without laughing.

"Dude, it doesn't have to be monumental. How is the breakfast thing different than counting our steak and lobster dinners?"

"Yeah, you're right. I'm just being a dick."

Cooper continues, "I mean, our to-do lists here are going to be limited. But you have to have things to look forward to, things to try, to do...anything to keep your mind busy. Sitting around and pining over what you wish you could do would make anyone feel insane."

"How do you handle the fear?"

"Like, the fear of dying?" he questions.

"For starters, I guess."

"I'm not afraid to die, Berk."

I skeptically look at him.

"I'm not." He chuckles. "Honest. I mean, do I *want* to die? Of course not. But I've always just thought that I'll die when I'm meant to. If I were meant to die tomorrow, I would die tomorrow whether I was here or not. The manner in which I'd go would vary if I were back home, but the end result would be the same. There's no sense in worrying about it."

"But what about the people you'll leave behind? I suppose that's what I'm more worried about."

"It would suck for them, no doubt. But they would heal. They would move on. No one is guaranteed tomorrow, Berkeley. You know that better than anyone. But what I think you haven't grasped is that you have no control over it. It's going to be the way it's going to be—good or bad. You just have to make the best out of it. If I die, you'd better not spend a second being sad, questioning it, or playing the what-if game. You got it?"

"Same goes for if I die," I respond.

"Oh, I wouldn't fret one bit." His face looks smug.

"You're a dick."

He laughs. "You know I love ya, man."

"What about the fear of Maggie leaving you?"

"I don't worry about it. It follows the same general principle. Maggie's not going to leave me, and if she does, she would have anyway. Nothing I can do about it."

"That's kind of depressing."

"No," he disagrees. "It's actually the opposite. It's more freeing than anything. When you get that all the worrying isn't going to change the end result, you can let it all go. When you realize that you have little control over the outcome of your life, you can stop spending so much energy trying to control it…and just live it."

I'm quiet for a moment, pondering over what Cooper said. "You know my entire existence is focused on control, right?"

"I do, and I'm telling you to let that part go."

"Easier said than done."

"Maybe, but you can try. All change has to start somewhere."

"You know, you kind of freak me out when you go all Oprah on me."

"Dude, you know I can't help it. I was raised in a house with four women. Chicks love to give advice. It kind of goes with the territory."

"You're still weird."

"I never said I wasn't." Cooper chuckles.

"You ready to go get some chow?"

"Yes, I'm starving."

"So, what new thing are you going to try today?" I question in an overly excited voice.

Cooper ignores my obvious stab and answers seriously, "I'm thinking blueberries. You know I never really get fruit with my breakfast. Maybe I should. Plus, I read that blueberries help your memory and shit. So, maybe it will stop me from getting Alzheimer's later in life?"

I laugh as we walk to the mess hall. "You're something else."

"What about you?" he asks.

"What about me what?"

"What are you going to try?"

I squint, cynically eyeing him.

"Just play along," he urges.

"I suppose I'll get sausage today since I normally get bacon. How's that?"

"Eh, it's a start." Cooper shakes his head, and I can't help but laugh.

NINETEEN

London

"I don't want to change who I am. I mean, I love me, but awesomeness is infinite, so I can always become even more awesome."
—London Wright

I'm stirring. I'm stirring. What does it say again?

I look over to the cookbook lying open on the granite counter. *"Simmer until sauce thickens."*

Has it thickened? How thick are we talking here?

The sauce bubbles in the pan.

I'm quite impressed with myself. I've been trying to use my time, sans Loïc, for a little self-improvement. I don't want to change who I am. I mean, I love me, but awesomeness is infinite, so I can always become even more awesome. So, that is my worthy goal—to become a better version of myself.

One of my projects is to become a better cook—or, let's face it, a cook, period. Based on the looks of this sauce, I'm rocking it.

"Whatcha making?" Paige comes bounding into our kitchen in her new business suit. The soft gray pencil skirt makes her ass and legs look amazing.

"You look hot today," I say. "I bet that Tom guy was all over you."

Tom's one of Paige's coworkers, and he's been trying to get her to go on a date with him for the last month.

"He did come into my office quite a bit today." She sets her purse down at the end of the counter, opens the cupboard above it, and pulls out a wine glass. "Want a glass?" she asks.

"Sure."

She grabs a bottle of wine from the refrigerator.

I ask, "Tom's cute, right?"

"Yeah, very," she says, pouring two generous glasses of wine.

She hands me a glass, and I take a sip before setting it down.

"So, why won't you go out with him again?"

"You know what they say. *Don't bite the hand that feeds you.*"

"That doesn't make sense," I argue.

"It makes total sense."

"No, it doesn't. That means, like, don't say bad things about your boss, not don't date a coworker."

"Well, you know what they say. *The squeaky wheel gets the grease.*" She takes a big gulp of wine. "This is so good. What brand is it?"

"It's that one we got from the wine tasting at that cute little winery in Tecumseh."

"Oh, right. Well, we need to go back there."

"Sure," I agree. "But, anyway, that saying makes no sense either. So, stop talking in ill-guided proverbs and just tell me why you won't give a hot, successful guy a chance." I take a bite of a spaghetti noodle that I just scooped up from a pot of boiling water. *Seems done to me.*

"Because, London, I really like this job. I don't want to screw it up by dating a coworker, only to have things go south and work be awkward. You know?"

I pour the pot of noodles and steaming water into a strainer in the sink. "You're not getting any younger, Paige. If a guy like Tom comes along and wants to take you out, you should let him."

"OMG, you're a weirdo. I'm twenty-three, not forty-three. I think I've got time." Paige huffs. "Look at you, Mrs. Love Expert. Just because you're in your first real relationship—"

"I'm bored! I miss Loïc! I need a project. Look at me. I'm learning how to cook, for God's sake. I need help!" I gesture toward the stove, which is completely covered in red splatters.

Paige looks between me and the stove and starts laughing loudly. I can't help but join in. I barely recognize myself at the moment. I hate cooking.

"Why are you cooking?" she asks once her laughter subsides.

"I've already written all my articles for the week. I've cleaned. I even worked out."

"Wow," Paige says in an exaggerated tone.

"Exactly, so I figured I'd start teaching myself how to cook. It's kind of an important skill to have. Someday, I'll have a family, and I should know how to feed them." I shrug.

"We had all this stuff?" Paige gestures from the pots to the strainer in the sink.

I shake my head. "No, I had to go buy all of it."

"You are bored." She chuckles.

"I know."

"Well, your birthday's in less than two weeks. What do you want to do for it? The big two three." She holds up two fingers on one hand and three on the other, smiling like a goofball.

"I guess we can just do the normal dinner and then a club. We should invite Maggie."

"Sure, I'll text her and the rest of the girls. You know Dana was telling me about that totally nude male strip club in Canada. She went there for a bachelorette party and said it was so fun. We could get a hotel and party over the border? Something different."

"Eh, I think I'll pass. A club without floppy penises is preferred." I scrunch up my nose.

Paige shakes her head. "You are the lamest twenty-two-year-old I know."

"Hey! I resent that! I'm almost twenty-three." I stick out my tongue.

"All right, Grandma. So, are you gonna tell me what you cooked up for us?"

"Okay, well, I thought I would start with something simple. So, this is just a basic marinara sauce and noodles." I grab a teaspoon of the sauce and hold it out for Paige to taste.

She takes the spoonful in her mouth, and her face puckers up, her eyes squinting, as she swallows. "That's disgusting, London!"

"It is not!"

"It is! It tastes like an ashtray. I think you burned it."

"That's mean," I protest, dipping the spoon back into the pot to stir some more.

"It's the truth!" Paige argues back.

Taking the spoon from the sauce, I point it toward Paige. "You could at least pretend to like it."

A glob of marinara from the spoon splatters onto Paige's new suit jacket.

"Uh," she gasps loudly, her hands covering her mouth in shock.

"I'm so—"

Before I can finish my apology, Paige digs her fingers into the noodles in the strainer in the sink, and she lobs a huge handful at my face. The slimy pasta slithers down my cheeks.

"Rude!" I dip the spoon in the sauce again and launch its red contents toward Paige. It's a direct hit to her chest.

Before I realize what's happening, the kitchen is filled with flying noodles, red sauce zooming through the air, and many high-pitched shrieks.

"Stop it!"

"You stop it!"

"You're such a hooker!" Paige yells.

"You're a hooker," I retort.

Suddenly, the two of us are lying on the tiled floor, surrounded by the marinara massacre, laughing hysterically.

"Look! Spaghetti angels!" Paige exclaims as her hands and feet start moving out and back in, like she's making a snow angel.

Lying on my back, I start to move my arms and legs in the same motion. My sides ache with laughter as tears roll down my sticky cheeks.

Eventually, our momentary insanity ceases, and the two of us stand up to admire our angels.

"Can't say I've ever seen a better spaghetti marinara angel." Paige nods in approval.

"I concur." Looking to her, I start to giggle again as I take in her appearance.

She's covered in red splotches, and there are entire noodles draped over her shoulders and entangled in her hair.

"You owe me a new outfit," Paige says.

"I do. I totally do. We'll go shopping this weekend." I chuckle.

"I don't want to clean this up." She sighs.

"I'll hire a cleaning company."

"That's not very responsible of us." Paige raises a brow while scrunching up her lips.

"Eh," I say, making a noncommittal sound. "I don't know about you, but I've already grown a lot today. I actually exercised on purpose and cooked. My brain can take only so much growing per day."

"Do you think the red stains are going to come off the walls?" She motions to our white-painted walls.

"You know…I've been thinking that we need some color in here. I could call a painter, too?"

"Yeah!" Paige says excitedly. "Can we do that light gray-blue color?"

"Oh, that'll be so pretty. Definitely." I nod.

"Thai?"

"Yeah, let's go to the new place on Fourth. They have the best sesame chicken noodles."

"Sounds delish. Let's leave right after we shower. I didn't get a lunch break today. I'm starving," Paige says before she heads off to her bathroom.

I take one last look at the kitchen and shake my head. A huge grin spreads across my face as I head toward my room.

To: Loïc Berkeley

From: London Wright

Subject: Question 43

Hey, baby. I'm attaching pictures of our new kitchen. Isn't it pretty? Paige and I had a food fight with bright red sauce last week, and I had to hire a painter. I bet you thought I was going to say, *Just kidding*, but I'm not. Lol. It's the truth. But, to be honest, the kitchen was due for a makeover. I just love the new colors. The blue hues are so pretty and calming. It's my favorite room in the house now. And, since I'm rarely in the kitchen, that's not cool, so I've decided to remodel my entire house. Yay!

Don't judge. ;-)

You make your daily checklists like Cooper taught you, and I'm going to remodel a perfectly good house for no reason, other than I'm bored. We all cope in different ways. Plus, just think, when you get back, it's going to be so exciting for you to see all the newly redecorated rooms.

So, I'm trying to figure out what to do for my birthday. I mean, twenty-three...it's kind of a big deal. I'm totally kidding. It so is not. But, still, you're not here, and that makes me sad, so I need to do something fun to cheer me up. Do you think you could sneak me into your base over there? You just say the word, and I'll hop on the next plane. ;-) Otherwise, maybe I'll go to Vegas or somewhere with Georgia and Paige for the weekend. I'm just not in the mood to go clubbing here. I'm over it. Maybe we'll go to a spa for the weekend. OMG...that is my mother's favorite thing to do on her birthday. I'm totally turning into her. Just great.

Well, to get to your last question, I get why you said Saturn. All those rings are pretty impressive, and as a child, I would have said Saturn, too. But, now, I'm going to have to say Pluto. You know why? Because Pluto is little and cute and has never caused problems. And people—whoever they are, those scientists somewhere—want to say that Pluto isn't a planet anymore, and I'm saying, WRONG. Pluto is totally still a planet, and that's why it's my favorite. Screw those people. What do they know?

So, question 43: Who's your favorite superhero? I'm saying Captain America. I'm not sure why. There's just something hot about him. Maybe it's the military thing? I mean, you're way hotter, of course. But, if I had to choose, I'd say him. What about you?

I hope you're safe. I hope you're happy. I hope you know how much I love you.

Love,

London

TWENTY

Loïc

"It feels like the calm before the storm. And life has taught me that storms aren't just damaging; they're devastating."
—*Loïc Berkeley*

I toss another gummy bear into my mouth. *Red, my favorite.* I'm lying on what can only be described as a military beanbag. Some soldier before me fashioned it by wrapping a tarp around a pile of straw and maybe some old clothes. I'm not certain, but it's comfortable enough.

I've never been a huge gummy bear fan, but that all changed when I met London. Now, I love them. I'm sure a lot of their appeal has to do with the nostalgic value they carry. These little sugary dudes remind me of London with every bite. Maybe that's why she sent them to me.

I just received my second care package from London. It was full of every flavor and shape of gummy that's sold along with gum, some snacks, replacements of all my favorite brands of toiletries, a Blu-ray player, a handful of Blu-ray movies, and a stack of pictures of London and me.

A bunch of my brothers and I are seated around the TV in our makeshift game room, watching *Deadpool*—one of the movies London sent—for the third time this week. London's so thoughtful. I'm glad she thought to send the Blu-ray player because all that was here prior to that was an old DVD player. Although the quality of the discs is lost on this crappy TV, it still gives us something to do.

Our game room is basically a rectangular shack made out of cheap plywood. It houses a few card tables, a TV, and a couple of couches. During my downtime, if I'm not at the gym, running, or in my room, I'm here. It's just a place to shoot the shit, watch a movie, play a game of cards, or just hang with some of the guys.

Cooper plops down on the couch next to me. "*Deadpool* again, huh?" He was late for the movie selection because he was finishing up Skyping with Maggie.

"Yep…that was the consensus."

"Cool." He reaches his hand toward my lap, plunges it into the bag of gummies, and pulls out a handful.

"How's Maggie?"

"She's great. She's been picking up all sorts of overtime to help pay for the wedding, which is cool."

"How are the wedding plans going?"

"Pretty good, I guess. I mean, she has a color-coded binder with information about everything from venue to cake to flowers and pictures as well. She seems pretty on top of things. I just sound excited when she tells me some new detail and agree with her when she asks my opinion. My job's pretty easy in this whole planning deal." He rests his head back into the couch, his eyes facing the TV.

"Well, aren't you?" I scoff.

"What?" He rolls his head to the side to face me.

"Excited."

"To marry Maggie? Of course. But the details don't really matter to me. I just want her to be happy. I don't care where we do it, who's there, what types of flowers she carries, or what music's playing as long as we're married at the end of it." He turns his head back toward the TV. "The wedding's great and all, but the real gift is the marriage. It's the lifetime. That's what I'm excited for."

"Yeah," I answer absentmindedly. I think about a lifetime with London and realize it doesn't freak me out in the least. In fact, the thought is kind of amazing.

Our brother Smith takes a seat on the couch next to Cooper. "Hey, Berk, Coops," he greets us. "You know this is the third time we're watching this one, right?"

"Yep," I answer.

"Your girl sent, like, twenty discs, right?"

"Yep." I grin. "It's what the masses voted for, dude. You gotta get here in time for the vote."

"I'm gonna have to." He leans back. "At least it's a good one."

"True," I agree.

I stare at the TV screen and find myself saying the lines from the movie in my head before Deadpool says them. "I think I'm going to hit the gym again," I say to Cooper, realizing it'd be a better use of my time.

"Okay. I'll come." He stands and follows me out of the rec building.

"I have a weird feeling," I mention as we exit the building.

"About?"

"I'm not sure exactly. It's just been awfully quiet around here lately. I feel like something's due to go down."

The insurgents have been distant. Our recon missions into the local villages the past couple of weeks have been completely by the book, no surprises whatsoever. There haven't been any rockets launched toward the base in a while, not even ones that hit outside the wire. It's been eerily still, and that's not normal. It feels like the calm before the storm. And life has taught me that storms aren't just damaging; they're devastating.

"Yeah, I know what you mean. One of the worst things about being here is waiting for the next attack. It puts us on alert, is all. I don't think we're any more likely to run into trouble just because it's been quiet. The trouble will find us at some point, regardless."

"Yeah, I know. It just makes me feel edgy."

"What doesn't make you feel edgy, dude?" Cooper's deep laugh permeates the cold night air.

"Asshole," I say with mock annoyance.

"So, Maggie tells me the Skype sex is going well with you and London." Cooper changes the subject.

"You've got to be kidding me." I shake my head.

"I have to say, I'm a little hurt that I have to hear it from my girlfriend who heard it from yours."

I laugh. "Dude, not everyone is an oversharer like you are."

"It wouldn't hurt to give me something. I mean, I talk your ear off all day, and you can't even throw me a bone?" Cooper jokes.

"Exactly! With all of your sharing, is there really time for me to talk?"

"You know I was kidding. I don't really talk that much."

"You talk more than I do," I offer.

"Who doesn't?" Cooper chuckles.

"True." I grin.

"Actually, I take that back," Cooper states. "This deployment, you've shared more than you ever have. It's kind of disturbing really. I don't know if it's London or this country that has you all worked up, but some conversations, I can't even believe it's you."

"I hear ya. I'm disturbing myself. It's like the floodgates have been broken, and now, I'm this oversharing fool...like you."

"You see, I know you meant that as a jab, but I took it as nothing but a compliment." Cooper shoots me a grin.

"I can't even remember what we were talking about."

"Skype sex."

I ignore his comment. "No, my weird feeling."

"There you go, talking about your feelings again."

"I'm gonna kick your ass,"

"I love ya, too, bro," Cooper responds before punching me in the arm.

After the gym and another shower, I open my laptop to type out a quick email to London before heading to bed. I find one from her in my inbox. Besides Skyping with her, there is no better feeling than the one I get from seeing her name pop up when I open my email.

To: Loïc Berkeley

From: London Wright

Subject: Question 49

Loïc,

My favorite exercise? You know I hate exercising! I'm not surprised that yours is running. I would have guessed that. I'm going to have to say Zumba. I've never done it, but I think I'd like it. It's like dancing. Who doesn't like dancing?

Wait a minute! Sex is totally exercise, right? Forget Zumba. Sex with you is the only exercise I need, and it's totally a workout.

Tomorrow's my birthday, as you know. ;-) I think we're just going to go out to a piano bar with a group of girls.

I was thinking of doing a spa weekend with my mom, Georgia, and Paige, but my mom is in Europe with my dad on business, and Georgia has to study for some exam.

Then, I thought for a moment about doing something fun, like an all-inclusive resort in Mexico or some other cool destination, but I feel like we just got back from LA, and honestly, it wasn't the most fun. So, Michigan, it is.

Yay.

Going to new places without you is kind of depressing. The entire time I'm there, I'm thinking, "Oh, Loïc would love this." Or, "I wonder if Loïc has been here before." It's weird, annoying, and slightly pathetic. But I just can't help it.

I'm hoping that, as time goes by, this year will get easier, you know? It has to.

Part of me thinks I'm an idiot for being so infatuated with someone I've only known for nine months. But I don't even care. I can't help the way I feel. I believe my feelings. I know they're real. I know I love you. And there's no guidebook on how to love or miss someone. Some of my feelings might lean toward obsession. But who am I to judge myself? Lol. It is what it is.

I love you. I miss you. I'm lost (metaphorically) without you. I don't handle being without you well. I suppose you can add it to my flaw list, but if I'm going to have a flaw, it's a good one to have. Without it, it would mean that there's no you...and that would never be acceptable.

You know what else? Who thought of this question game? We're on 49, and

I'm drawing a blank. Do you know how hard it is to come up with so many questions for someone you already know pretty well in the first place? It's difficult. I have no idea how I'm going to come up with new material when we're in the hundreds. There are going to be some pretty random questions at that point.

So, in honor of the randomness to come, here's question 49: What kind of sheets do you like? You know, there's flannel, silk, T-shirt, cotton, and so on. I ask because I'm sitting here in bed with my laptop on my lap, exhausted and ready to climb into my soft satin sheets to go to sleep. I love my sheets. Satin is my answer because, to me, they are perfect.

I love you, Loïc. Stay safe.

Love,

London

God, I adore her.

I love Skyping with her for so many reasons. Obviously, I get to see her face, hear her voice, and have a live back-and-forth conversation. But I truly love her emails. They are just so...her. They're funny, sweet, random, whiny, and incredibly adorable all at once...just like she is. I can almost hear her saying the words as she's typing, and though it's not the same as a live chat, I definitely feel closer to her after I've finished reading one.

She's brilliant, plain and simple. *And she's mine.* That thought will never get old.

I start to type my response.

To: London Wright

From: Loïc Berkeley

Subject: Question 50

London,

Sheets are sheets. And, for what it's worth, to me, you are perfect. But, I suppose, if I'm going to answer your question, I have to say satin as well because my vote will always be whatever type of sheet is covering you Who's pathetic now? ;-)

It'll probably be after midnight, my time, when you get this email, so...HAPPY BIRTHDAY, BABY! January 22 will forever be one of my favorite days because it was the day your beautiful, spunky, spoiled, sexy ass came into the world.

You're right. It sucks that we have to miss all of our first holidays together. I wish I were back in Michigan or in the locale of your choice to celebrate with you. I'm sure the piano bar with Paige and the girls will be fun. You've had a blast at your other twenty-two birthdays, I'm positive, so don't let my absence stop you from having fun at this one.

It's late, and I have to get up early, so I'm going to go. I'm free tomorrow between 1–2 p.m., your time. So, try to be on around one, and we'll Skype. I'd love to at least see your gorgeous face on your birthday.

Question 50: In your history of birthdays, which one was your favorite?

I think mine would have to be my seventh birthday. I've told you about it before, I believe. First, it was the last birthday that I celebrated with my parents. I got this awesome red mountain bike that I wanted so much at the time. My mom was happy. When I think about that day, feelings of joy come back to me. I actually dreamed about it the other day, which was weird. I don't know why. Maybe it was because of all our talk about your birthday and mine coming up next month. Plus, the memory of that day is pretty clear, whereas my earlier birthdays are fuzzier, getting more unclear the younger I was. So, anyway, that's mine.

Remember, 1 p.m., your time.

I love you, London.

Happy birthday, baby.

Love,

Loïc

TWENTY-ONE

Loïc

*"Perhaps I fell in love with her not because of one moment,
but because every moment led me to her."*
—Loïc Berkeley

It's killing me that I don't have time to check my laptop
before we head out, but I don't. I've grown what I might
classify as an unhealthy dependence on that device. It's as
close as I've ever been to an addiction in my life. I live for
communication from London. I crave it. Truthfully, that
brilliant little machine is getting me through this
deployment. Let's face it; I'm already an addict, and
London's my drug of choice.

I don't know when it all happened. *When did lust
become interest? Interest become adoration? Adoration become love?
Love become all-consuming need?* It's so strange. I feel like, one
minute, I was trying to avoid this insistent girl named
London, and the next, I was head over heels in love with
her. I can't pinpoint the instant that it all happened.

Maybe it wasn't even a specific minute in time? Perhaps I fell in love with her not because of one moment, but because every moment led me to her. Each second that I've spent with London has contributed to the overwhelming way in which I love her now.

Me, Loïc Berkeley, in love. Obviously, I've known for months that I've felt this way about London. Yet I don't think I realized the gravity—the all-encompassing nature of it all—until I got here, and I couldn't see her, touch her, and feel her every day. Her absence solidified everything for me. It's only London. It will only ever be London.

I'm twenty-six, as of yesterday, and I will never want another woman in my life. Oddly, I'm completely okay with that.

Pounding sounds on my door.

"Berk! We're out!"

I've just finished putting on the last of my gear, so I grab my gun and open the flimsy door of my room.

"Ready," I greet Cooper as I exit.

It's three in the morning. The sun won't rise for another three and a half hours.

I jump up into the armored Humvee with the rest of the guys. We're heading out for a mission in Sarowbi, which is about an hour away, just east of Kabul. We received intel late yesterday that an Al-Qaeda general, who is responsible for killing at least twenty Marines in the past several months, has a safe house there. Chances are, he's long gone by now, and this is going to strictly be a reconnaissance mission where we'll collect any intel we can from anyone willing to talk about the general's current location. However, we're getting there early, before the sun rises, to either capture the general or to startle some local Afghans with a scary wake-up call.

As far as missions go, this one has uneventful written all over it. The intel we received was too scattered and random. It leads me to believe it's either old or incorrect information. More than likely, today's going to be a glorified field trip to Sarowbi, which is a pretty boring little village.

"Dude, birthday Skype sex?" Cooper whispers next to me so that only I can hear over the rumble of the truck's engine.

"What is your obsession with that?" I look to him, raising an eyebrow in confusion.

The deep timbre of his laughter resonates through the back of the vehicle. "Dude, you know I only keep asking because it makes you all uncomfortable and shit. It's hilarious."

"Hilarious," I deadpan with a roll of my eyes. "If you want to know that bad, it was fucking awesome. The best Skype sex I've had since I've been here. Happy?"

"Nice! Some kick-ass birthday virtual sex. London's a keeper." He nods his head in approval.

"She is," I agree.

"Did you get a chance to Skype with Maggie yesterday?"

Maggie works all sorts of odd shifts at the hospital. I've long stopped trying to keep up with her schedule. It's easier just to ask Cooper.

"I did. She was off last night."

"Sweet. How is she?"

"Great. Do you remember that broad Patricia?" Cooper asks.

"Um…" I run the name over in my head, trying to recall who she is.

"You know, that tall, busty brunette friend Maggie had in college. Remember she always used to call you Loh-Key?"

Realization dawns. "Ugh, I hated her."

"I know, right? Well, she contacted Maggie out of the blue yesterday. Apparently, she had heard from someone that we were getting married and was pissed that she hadn't been asked to be a bridesmaid. She hasn't spoken to Maggie in probably two years. Even when they were friends, she was such a bitch to Maggie. Honestly, Maggie wasn't planning on inviting her ass, let alone asking her to be a bridesmaid. Isn't it weird how delusional some people are?"

"She was always so stuck on herself. God, I hated that bitch." I shake my head, trying to rid my mind of the memories of Patricia.

"She was. Well, you know how Maggie is with confrontation. She basically tried to explain to Patricia that she wasn't invited to the wedding in a way that wouldn't hurt her feelings."

"How'd that go?" I smile, thinking of sweet Maggie and her inability to be mean to anyone, even those who deserve it.

"Not good."

"No? So, Patricia's going to be at the wedding?" God, listening to myself, I sound like a gossipy college girl.

"Hell no. Maggie told her the wedding was two weeks after it's actually planned. Then, she's going to forget to send her an invite and block Patricia's angry calls after the fact."

"Sounds like a plan." I chuckle. "What else is going on back home?"

I lean back and listen to Cooper fill me in on the news pertaining to his sisters and parents and other friends of Maggie's. None of it is that interesting or particularly relevant to our lives here, but his words are soothing in an odd way.

Talk of normalcy and home is like a lullaby for soldiers. It's a quiet reminder of why we're here, why we're fighting. The life that we all take for granted when we're in it is actually the pot of gold at the end of the rainbow. Living a life that is so ordinary is a true gift, one worth defending at all costs.

We park by the mountain's edge on the outskirts of Sarowbi. As soon as we exit the vehicle, all side conversations are over, and we're completely concentrated on the task at hand. Even though, more than likely, this is going to be a giant waste of time, we never execute a mission without putting one hundred percent of our focus toward it. Surprises happen, and here, they aren't good things, so we must always be ready and alert.

Putting on our night goggles, we make our way on foot through the darkness at the base of the mountain. A surveillance stop on the outskirts of the village doesn't show anything suspicious, so we continue forward until we're standing outside our destination. It's a small home that looks like it was made out of clay from the earth. The holes for the windows are covered by fabric curtains on the inside and nothing more. If the general chose to seek protection here, he mustn't be very bright. That, or he has very little options. There are two doors, one in the front and the other in the back.

We quickly take our positions, armed and ready.

On cue, we enter the building. Screams of surprise and confusion sound through the glorified hut as we point our weapons toward the occupants. After a diligent inspection of those inside, we realize our target is definitely not among them. Our translator stays along with a couple of armed soldiers, and the rest of us exit the home and await further instructions outside.

"Surprise, surprise," Cooper says to me as we exit.

"I know. I had a feeling it would be a wild goose chase."

"Me, too."

A half hour later, when the soldiers emerge from the house, the sun is up, and the village people are starting to rise and start their day.

"It turns out, he was here, in the village, though the family in this home says he didn't stay with them. They also state that they haven't seen him in a couple of weeks but that someone in this village is bound to know something," Captain Ismirle informs our unit. "Berkeley and Cooper, take your guys down the south side of the street. Stop at each house, and see what you can find." He addresses one of our military translators, "Liles, you can go with them." He turns to a lieutenant leading another unit. "Parker, take your guys to the houses on the north side. Let's see what we can find."

We get started. Not surprisingly, none of the residents want to talk to us, and they are hesitant to give us any information. I don't blame them. If anyone from Al-Qaeda found out that they helped us, they would wind up dead. We never leave these types of missions with much intel to speak of. A lot of what we do is not only listening to what the people of the village say, but also taking in all the details of their homes, looking for weapons or clues.

Around mid morning, we enter another home, in which the residents once again swear they have no information. As Liles continues to speak with them,

Cooper nudges my boot with his. I turn to him, and he nods toward the back room. I immediately notice the rug that's on the floor. I can't explain it, but something's off about it.

We walk to the back room, and I kick at the rug with my boot. Sure enough, a door is revealed. We look around the small room before Cooper bends to open the wooden door in the floor while I cover him. Inside the hidden compartment, we find IEDs, mortar rockets, other explosives, and a bunch of machine guns.

"Oh, they know something." Cooper shakes his head.

"They sure do," I agree.

We head the few steps back into the front room to find the Afghan family gone.

"Where'd they go?" I question, instinctual fear causing the hairs on the back of my neck to rise.

"They said they wanted to show us something outside. Liles took them out." Jacoby nods toward the door.

"What?" Cooper asks. "That doesn't even make sense."

"I know," Smith answers. "Liles seemed confused, too. He was thinking maybe he was missing something in the translation, so he wanted them to show him what they were talking about."

"The woman kept looking down," Jacoby adds. "I don't trust her."

"Yeah, well, she definitely knows something. We found an entire arsenal of weapons in the floor in the back room." Cooper points to the back room.

"No shit!" our brother Nader exclaims.

"Let's go give Liles backup, and then we'll come back to figure this out," I say right before a dark object flies in through the open window and drops on the floor. "Run!" I shout, knowing instantly that it's a grenade.

They say that the seconds before you die play out in slow motion, and they're right. In a matter of seconds, more thoughts than I thought were possible run through my mind.

I immediately take stock of my surroundings. The exits are both farther than a few seconds away. The sobering fact that we'll never be able to clear a doorway before it explodes enters my thoughts.

We're going to die.

The guys, four of my brothers, have lives, families, and loved ones.

Maybe some of us will make it?

I think of Cooper, my true brother, and the wedding that he might not be able to attend. Finally, I think of my beautiful London and how very much I'm going to miss her.

My eyes find Cooper's, and in them, I see determination, regret, and love. His stare communicates so much, but it takes me a fraction of a second too long to realize what.

I yell, "No!" as my arm reaches out for him even though I know he's not within my reach.

I lunge toward him as I watch him fall on the grenade.

The explosive beneath his body detonates. I stare in horror as Cooper's body comes apart and shatters into pieces, tearing through the air. I'm off my feet and flying backward, but I'm unable to take my eyes off of my friend, my brother. Debris flies toward me, but I don't feel it hit me.

I can't feel anything.

As I collide with a hard surface behind me and I fall to the ground, everything fades to black. So many emotions are ripping me to pieces, but the last thought that burns through my mind before the darkness pulls me under is that I hope I never feel anything again.

TWENTY-TWO

London

"Love is crazy. It turns sane, independent people into wide-eyed, mushy-hearted saps. And I love it."
—London Wright

I like how, every time I open my email, the question number gets larger in the subject line. It's not an accurate count as to how many days I've been without Loïc. When he's gone on multiple-day missions, he can't send an email, and then some days, we are able to send more than one question back and forth. So, it's not precise in keeping track of the days gone by, but it's actually kind of averaging out to almost one question a day. I get an intense feeling of joy when I see the question number in the comment line of each new email. It's like the larger the number, the closer I am to seeing him again.

Loïc's been gone two and a half months, and although I wouldn't say it's getting easier to be apart from him, it's becoming less difficult—if that makes any sense at all. I guess I'm able to manage my feelings better and control the agonizing longing my heart feels for him. I'm trying to keep myself busy, which helps, too.

My heart falls when I open my email and see that I don't have a new one from him. The last one was from two days ago, February 20, Loïc's twenty-sixth birthday. I do what I always do when I don't find a new email from him, I re-read the last one he sent.

To: London Wright

From: Loïc Berkeley

Subject: Question 80

I don't know. My seventh birthday might have been overtaken by my twenty-sixth. Our Skype session earlier was amazing, London. The only thing that would have been more amazing was if I could have been home with you, but we've got next year, right?

To answer your question, yes, I've jumped out of airplanes. I wouldn't call it skydiving exactly, but I think it counts. I've actually jumped out of many airplanes and helicopters. It's part of my training, part of what I do. But I will gladly take you skydiving when I'm home. I'd love to experience that first with you.

I'm possibly going to be gone all day tomorrow. I'll write when I'm back.

I have a very early wake-up call, so I'm going to sign off.

So, question 80 is kinda deep. What's your greatest regret?

I know I've told you how I want to find Nan and Granddad when I get back. Well, now that my heart isn't filled with so much hurt and hate, I regret not trying to find them earlier. As soon as I get back from our mission, I'm going to use some of my downtime here to look them up. You know, I think you're right. Something must have happened.

It's taken loving you for me to realize that. I know now that, when you really love someone, you would never just abandon them without reason. I believe in my heart that they truly loved me when I was little. Even as a young boy, I felt their love. It was real.

So, something must have happened. There must be a reason, I think. Don't you?

Gotta go to bed.

I love you, London.

Love,

Loïc

I read my response to him from yesterday.

To: Loïc Berkeley

From: London Wright

Subject: Question 81

Loïc,

Yes, of course I feel that something happened. It had to have. It just doesn't make sense that grandparents would abandon their only grandchild. I believe that there was something that stopped them from getting you. Maybe something legal? I'm not sure how all of that works. But the fact that they were in a different country had to present problems.

I think that whatever you find in regard to them will be good for you to know. The mind can create scenarios that are much darker than the reality. Whatever you find out, you'll be okay. I just know it.

So, regrets? I hate this question because, as I go through my possible answers, none of them are as profound as yours. I know it's not a competition or anything, but it makes my life seem shallow. I suppose, in a way, it was...is? No, I'll stick with *was*.

It seems so unfair that I have to put so much effort into this question when your life presented you with such a deep regret. The truth is, I don't have many true regrets. Sure, there are things that I did or said that I'm not proud of. But I also know that each of those situations helped me grow as a person. I learned from every experience. Sometimes, the lesson might have taken longer than it should have to sink in, but I got it eventually.

I regret some of the silly fights I had with my mom or sister, but none of them had a lasting impact on my life. They were more about learning how to problem solve and mature. I've regretted opportunities that I didn't take or didn't work for. But all those missed opportunities brought me here, and I'm pretty darn happy with my life at the moment.

I wish I had talked to you about "cheating on me" last summer before assuming the worst and heading to a bar with ill intentions. But, even with that event, we grew as a couple when we talked about it afterward.

So, I guess, I'm sticking with no regrets. That should be my hashtag. ;-)

Question 81: Do you have any random fears?

I don't think that I've told you that I'm afraid of fish. Yes, fish. I'm crazy, I know. Once, when I was little, my sister and I swam in a lake in Wisconsin, and a fish nibbled on my toes. It freaked me the hell out. It didn't really hurt, but it scared me. So, now, I'm afraid to swim in lakes where fish can nibble on me.

How about you?

I'm working on some job leads. I will let you know how they go.

Stay safe. I love you so very much, Loïc Berkeley.

Love,

London

#noregrets

After I finish reading my email, I go back to browsing the Internet. I opt to wait a while before writing him another email. I'm hoping he'll sign on any minute and we'll be able to Skype. I've been searching online the past few weeks for local journalism jobs or writing gigs that would allow me to write freelance articles and send them in remotely. Leaving Michigan is no longer an option. I might leave someday, but it'll be when Loïc comes with me. And I need a job with a little more challenges now.

I think I've tapped out my potential with the job I currently have.

I have moments when I think that maybe this is all moving too fast. I'm twenty-three, and I've already planned my entire life with Loïc. A year ago, that was not the plan. I was going to work, travel, hang with my girl Paige, and enjoy being young and single until at least thirty. *Who dreams of marriage before thirty anymore? Certainly not this girl. Well, until now.*

Now, it's all I think about—not marriage exactly…but an eternity with Loïc. *Who wouldn't want to settle down at twenty-three when they have Loïc at their side?* Love is crazy. It turns sane, independent people into wide-eyed, mushy-hearted saps. And I love it.

Obviously, I wanted Loïc at that car wash almost a year ago, but that was lust, plain and simple. He was hot, and I wanted to conquer him and have some fun…for just a bit. I wanted to win him even if just for a night, and then I would send him on his way. *Who knew that it would turn into so much more? Definitely not me.*

Love's amazing that way. It just kinda hits you, and when it's real love, it's for always. *How could it not be? In true love, forever is the only option.*

My phone chimes. Looking down toward it on the desk, I see Maggie's name lighting up the screen.

A smile crosses my face as I answer. Maggie and I have gotten close since the guys left.

"Hey!" I answer cheerfully.

Maggie's crying. My breath hitches.

Something's wrong.

The desperation in her sobs is palpable, and I'm instantly filled with dread.

"What's wrong? Tell me. What is it?" I beg, not able to take not knowing for one more second.

"He's…he's dead, London," she says through broken cries.

I freeze. Big streams of tears course down my cheeks. I release the breath that I didn't realize I had been holding.

"Who?" I ask hesitantly even though I'm not ready to hear the answer.

She sucks in air between sobs and chokes out, "David."

"No!" I scream, hysterical now. "No! No! No! Are you sure? No!"

She doesn't respond to my nonsensical cries with her words, instead letting out wails of utter heartache and devastation. I've never heard such tangible sounds of pain before. Maggie's miles away, yet I feel her despair weighing down on me, like a blanket of sadness.

We continue to cry together on the phone. I have no words. I don't even know what to say. I'm so sad for her, for Loïc, and of course…for Cooper.

How could this have happened?

I see stories about deaths of soldiers on the news all the time. It's pretty commonplace in today's world. Typical responses—*That's too bad*, *That poor guy*, *He was so young*, or *His poor family*—go through my head when I hear of those incidences.

But to have that soldier be someone I know?

Devastation doesn't come close to describing the pain burning inside me.

I know Cooper.

I love Cooper.

His smile, his laugh, his sense of humor, the way in which he loves Maggie, his importance to Loïc—all of it coming together renders him irreplaceable. Every little thing that made him who he was makes this hurt so much.

There will never be another David Cooper in this world ever again.

I will feel his loss every day for the rest of my life.

I will never again hear his jokes, have him make me a delicious meal, or feel him pull me into a hug. I will never see a smile on Maggie's or Loïc's face that was put there by Cooper, and this maybe hurts the most.

A smile caused by Cooper is something precious. It was real, big, and infectious. When I saw someone smiling because of Cooper, I couldn't help but smile with them. Cooper's joy had a way of pulling everyone in and taking us all on a journey with him.

If one knew Cooper, they loved him. *How many people in the world can I say that about?*

I can think of only one—and now, he's gone.

He's gone.

Poor Maggie. I will mourn Cooper forever, but what about her? How will she go on?

"Wha-what happened?" My voice shakes.

"A grenade." Her words are barely audible, but I react as if she screamed them in my face.

I gasp, and my body recoils as I lean away from my phone. Yet no amount of distance between Maggie's voice and myself will make the words any less true. I squeeze my eyes shut as the thoughts of Cooper's body being blown up enter my mind.

I can't go there. Oh my God, I can't. No, no, no. I shake my head back and forth.

"I'm...so...sorry," I cry for lack of anything more profound to say.

Maggie's continued sobs are her only response.

I've been sitting in the same spot for at least an hour...maybe two? I haven't been able to move since hanging up with Maggie. The range of emotions that course through me are paralyzing. I'm still having a difficult time with believing that my phone conversation with Maggie actually happened. It's all so surreal, a freakish nightmare from which I desperately need to wake up from.

But, as much as I wish it were something my mind conjured up in my sleep, I know it's not. It's real.

Cooper's dead.

That knowledge carries so much sadness but also an equal amount of guilt. I think back to Maggie's phone call, and though I only felt it for less than a second, I can't pretend that I didn't feel relief when she said Cooper's name and not Loïc's. I'm an awful person. God, I'm so ashamed to admit it. I wish more than anything that Cooper were still alive, gracing the world with his warm smile and witty personality.

But, at the same time, I'm unable to ignore the immense relief I feel that Loïc's alive. It's not like I'm glad it was Cooper and not Loïc. That's not it at all. I wish it didn't have to be either of them. I wish more than anything that Maggie didn't have to be going through such pain.

My face feels stiff, the tears that dried on my skin making it feel taut. Tears no longer fall as I sit at my desk, motionless and in shock.

How could this have happened? How could this possibly be real?

As much as my heart hurts for Maggie, it breaks for Loïc. *What is this loss going to do to him? Was he there? God, I hope not.*

Loïc has lost so much, and now, he's lost his best friend. This is going to tear him apart. I think to the Loïc that I first met back in May with his closed-off, tough-asshole exterior meant to scare away anyone who wanted to get too close. *Will he go back to that place? Is he going to try to shut me out?*

No. I shake my head.

We've come too far. He isn't that person anymore. Sure, he'll be devastated, but we'll get through it together. We can get through anything as long as we're together.

I hate that I can't call him.

Maybe he'll be online. I open my laptop, but my hopes fall when I see the little circle next to his name is a sad gray and not the bright green I was praying to see.

An email will have to do.

To: Loïc Berkeley

From: London Wright

Subject: I'm so sorry.

Loïc,

I just heard about Cooper. I don't know what else to say besides I'm so, so very sorry. I wish I had something to say to make this better, but I know nothing will. I wish more than anything that it hadn't happened. I wish that you didn't have to go through the pain that I know you are feeling. I wish you were here right now, so I could hold you.

I love you, Loïc. We are going to get through this. You are going to get through this.

Please write when you can. I hate that I can't be with you right now.

Are they going to let you come home for the funeral?

I'm sorry. I wish I had something better to say that would help you, but I'm at a loss. All I know is that, as horrible as this is...we will get through it, Loïc. It won't always hurt this much.

I love you.

I'm sorry.

I'm so very sorry.

Love,

London

TWENTY-THREE

Loïc

TWENTY-FOUR

London

To: Loïc Berkeley

From: London Wright

Subject: Please call me.

Loïc,

I'm so sorry about Cooper, and I'm so worried about you. Please call me. We can get through this. You can get through this. Talk to me.

I love you.

Love,

London

TWENTY-FIVE

Loïc

TWENTY-SIX

London

To: Loïc Berkeley

From: London Wright

Subject: I love you.

Loïc,

I love you. I love you. I love you.

I can't wait to hold you.

It won't always hurt this much, I promise.

Please call me anytime, day or night. I don't care when. I can't imagine what you're going through, and I just need to talk to you.

Please call me.

I love you so very much.

Love,

London

TWENTY-SEVEN

Loïc

TWENTY-EIGHT

London

To: Loïc Berkeley

From: London Wright

Subject: I'm sorry.

Loïc,

I don't know what you're going through. But I know how much I'm hurting, and I can only imagine that you're hurting more. I wish I could take away your pain. I wish I could change things. But I can't.

I can be here for you and love you. I can promise you that we can get through this.

Please call me. I'm so worried about you.

I love you so much.

Love,

London

TWENTY-NINE

Loïc

THIRTY

London

To: Loïc Berkeley

From: London Wright

Subject: Love

Loïc,

I know I'm probably not saying the right words. I admit that I don't know what to say to ease some of your pain, if that is even possible. But I do know that I love you. While I might not do or say the correct things, I can love you with everything I am.

Love has the power to heal. I know it does.

I know it won't be tomorrow, next month, or maybe not even next year, but I will love you through all the pain until you're able to feel okay. I understand that you will always mourn Cooper, but someday, you'll be able to look back at the good times that you shared. Maybe, someday, every memory you have of him won't be tainted with sadness. Just maybe?

Please call me.

I love you so much.

Love,

London

THIRTY-ONE

Loïc

THIRTY-TWO

London

To: Loïc Berkeley

From: London Wright

Subject: Are you okay?

Loïc,

Are you okay? I mean, I know you're not okay, but you know what I mean.

Where are you? What's going through your mind? Please share your thoughts with me…whatever they are.

I'm sorry if I'm being selfish, but I need to hear from you. Anything. I'm going crazy, not knowing how you are. I'm terrified of you mourning the loss of Cooper over there by yourself.

Why aren't they sending you home? You can't possibly think clearly on missions with everything that's happened. Don't they understand that?

I get that what you're going through is way worse than what I am feeling. But I love you, and I'm worried sick about you. Maggie hasn't heard from you, and I don't know who else to check with.

Please don't shut me out. Please let me help you.

Please. Please. Please. Please. Please.

I love you, Loïc Berkeley, and nothing will ever change that.

Love,

London

THIRTY-THREE

Loïc

THIRTY-FOUR

London

"I have to focus on what I can control because nothing is more depressing than trying to change what I can't."
—*London Wright*

To: Loïc Berkeley

From: London Wright

Subject: Funeral

Loïc,

The funeral's tomorrow. Are they going to let you come home for it? Hopefully, you are already on your way. God, I hope so.

I need to see you. I don't know what else to say besides I love you.

I. Love. You.

Always. Always. Always.

Love,

London

Sitting on the padded bench in the bay window of my bedroom, I close my laptop.

I'm not good at this, this military life. *How do wives and girlfriends handle the stress of it all—the worry, the not knowing, the sadness, the anxiety…the despair?* It's all too much. It's suffocating. I can't function.

The days since Cooper's death have dragged on, each one an eternity in itself. I know I have to mourn Cooper, but I'm drowning in my worry for Loïc.

I just feel…lost.

I've always been successful at things in life that I've truly wanted. Yet, more than anything I've ever needed, I want to be able to navigate my days with grace instead of despair. But, no matter how much I try to find the strength, it's out of my reach every time.

No amount of money can buy feelings. But, if I could, I would cash in my entire trust fund for an ounce of peace. The lack of it is driving me crazy.

Leaning my head against the window, I watch as the wind whips frozen flurries around. The snowflakes travel in a frigid dance through the air. It's captivating and hauntingly sad. They're caught in the gusts of the bitter wind, unable to fall to the earth even if they wanted to.

Maybe, on another day, I would have found the swirls of white beautiful. But, today, all I see are flakes that are forced into a frenzy of movement, being denied the peace of the padded ground.

Soft knocks sound on my door before it opens gently.

"Hey," Paige says quietly.

Lifting my face from the window, I look to her. "Hey."

"I'm assuming no news?" She looks to me with pity.

"No." I shake my head. "I just wrote him again but still nothing from his end."

"He'll come around. Who knows what happens over there after a death? Maybe he doesn't have access to his laptop right now."

"Yeah, maybe," I say with little conviction.

Her face perks up, and she sings, "*The sun will come out—*"

"No." I adamantly shake my head. I am not in the mood for a reenactment from the movie *Annie*.

"*Tomorrow…*" she belts out.

"Stop, Paige. I'm serious," I warn.

"*Bet your bottom dollar that tomorrow, there'll be sun.*" She sashays toward me and grabs my hands, pulling me off of the bench.

Before I know it, I'm part of this freak show as we both sing out from the tops of our lungs, "*When I'm stuck with a day that's gray and lonely…*"

I hold my hands out to my sides, as if I were a Broadway performer, "*I just stick up my chin and grin and say, oh…the sun will come out tomorrow…*"

Paige and I dance around my room in our two-woman show, shrieking like a couple of dying cats in our personal Broadway performance of one of our favorite songs.

We pose and extend our jazz hands as we belt out as loud as we can the final note in a key that hasn't been invented yet.

I finally have to let the last note die when I need to stop to take a breath. I turn to Paige, both of us red in the face and sporting gigantic grins. My smile drops as the plump tears begin streaming down my face. Paige pulls me into her arms, and the two of us stand in my room while I cry.

I don't know how long I cry, but Paige's shirt is covered in tears and snot when I finally pull away and wipe my face with the arm of my shirt.

"Feel better?" she asks as she rubs the sides of my arms with her hands.

I nod my head.

"Good. You know what they say. *Sometimes, you just need to participate in a grand Broadway performance before having a good cry.*"

"No one says that." I chuckle.

"I do." She shrugs. "Let's go get some dinner. I'm starving."

"Yeah, me, too," I agree.

Paige leaves my room, and I look longingly at my laptop. I've been obsessively checking it ever since I got the call from Maggie. It's only been a half hour or so since I sent my last message, so I know there wouldn't be an email from Loïc anyway. For whatever reason, he's not ready to communicate yet, and I have to accept that.

Using all of my willpower, I walk away from the laptop and into my bathroom to wash my tear-streaked face. I remind myself that I'll have my phone to check for emails.

He'll write or call when he's ready. I can't dictate his behavior, but I can change mine. I need to change mine.

Living in a vacuum of misery while compulsively refreshing my inbox isn't healthy.

I might not be able to erase the worry altogether, but I can lessen it. I can join the land of the living. I can take showers, leave the house, and go to dinner with my best friend. I have to focus on what I can control because nothing is more depressing than trying to change what I can't.

Paige is right. I guess all I needed was a cheeky performance and a good cry.

THIRTY-FIVE

London

"Funerals suck. All of them blow. But this one sucks the most."
—*London Wright*

Today's the day—the last day of February—a day I've been dreading for so many reasons. I stroll arm in arm with Paige up the cement walkway toward the church. The salt crystals that were tossed onto the sidewalk are still intact as they crunch under my heels. The frigid temperature is too frigid for even the salt to melt the ice.

My fingers, though nestled in black leather gloves, are frozen. I can no longer feel the skin on my face as it's assaulted by the bitter air on this record-breaking cold day.

Today is truly miserable. Even the earth is mourning the loss of Cooper.

Once inside the church, Paige and I find a seat in a wooden pew. There's a casket covered with an American flag at the front of the church. Beside it is a large framed picture of Cooper in uniform, his all-American boy smile gracing his face. Even if one had never met Cooper, they would be sad to say good-bye to the man in that picture. His goodness shines out of the frame, reminding everyone here of the true tragedy of this loss.

The world is a little bit darker without the light that was David Cooper. I know people say that all the time about people when they die. But, with Cooper, it is so true. Everyone who knew him will forever be changed. We'll all be missing a sliver of joy, one that we'll never get back.

The first two rows are taken up by Cooper's and Maggie's families. The women, who I assume are Cooper's sisters, are hunched, their backs moving with silent cries, as they bring hands clutched with Kleenexes to their faces.

Then, there's Maggie, sitting between her parents, and though I can only see the back of her, the heartache in her posture is evident, and my heart aches for her.

Behind the rows of immediate family are military men in their dress uniforms, all sitting up straight, their posture communicating respect.

I scan the backs of the men for the one that I'm desperate to see. I haven't heard from Loïc since Cooper died. Unfortunately, Maggie hasn't either. I don't know if he was given permission to fly home for the funeral or not. I don't really know how that works. I'm sure, if a family member of a soldier passed while he was serving, he would be granted leave to return for the funeral. But a friend? I don't know. Cooper was so much more than a friend to Loïc, but perhaps, with the military, it's all black and white. I doubt the closeness or level of friendship is taken into account.

But maybe? I'm praying that he's here. I desperately need to see him.

I keep looking back to the door, praying to see Loïc walking through it, but when the priest starts the service, my hopes fall.

He's not coming. I can't believe it. He's not coming.

Paige wraps her arm around my shoulder and pulls me into her side, as if she knows I'm about to break. I lean my head onto her shoulder, thankful that she's here with me. My family offered to fly in for the funeral, but I told them that they didn't need to. They had never met Cooper, but they understood how important he was to me. But I knew I would have Paige here. She loved Cooper, and she is basically my family anyway.

This isn't the first funeral I've been to. I've been to quite a few actually—grandparents, great-aunts and great-uncles, and family friends.

Funerals suck. All of them blow. But this one sucks the most.

The other ones I've been to, although sad, were for older people, people who had lived a good life. Cooper didn't live a full life, not even close. He had so much more to do. His life was taken too soon, and the gravity of that injustice is almost unbearable.

I'm so sad, mad, heartbroken, and unbelievably furious that his life was cut short. It's not fair. I think that's why it's such a horrible loss.

Several people go up to the pulpit to say nice things about Cooper. I get it; we're here to celebrate his life. Yet it just makes me bitter. Hearing about how wonderful Cooper was causes me to be more upset that he's gone.

Finally, the service is over, and six men in their military dress uniforms walk to the front of the church. They pick up the casket and carry it down the aisle. The first two rows of Cooper and Maggie's closest family and friends follow the recession.

"I guess we go now," Paige says beside me as the people in our row begin to stand.

"Yeah."

Cooper's family and Maggie stand in the foyer of the church in a receiving line. We follow the line of people as they exit the church. I watch as Cooper's parents and sisters embrace each person who passes, extending thanks to those who came to celebrate Cooper's life.

What a miserable thing to have to do—console others when it is your son/brother/fiancé who died. I don't really understand this part of funerals. We should be the ones hugging and consoling them, not the other way around.

When I reach Maggie, we pull each other into a hug and cry. I didn't think I had any more tears left to cry, but they're falling again.

"I'm so sorry," I say when I finally pull away.

"I know. Me, too." Maggie nods. "Any news from Loïc?" she asks sadly.

"No. You?"

She shakes her head. "I wish he had been here. David would have wanted him here."

"I know." I nod.

"Let me know if you hear anything," she pleads softly.

"I will. You, too."

"Of course," she agrees. "Let's get together soon."

"Absolutely." I pull her into another hug before moving on to the next person in the receiving line.

I shake each of Cooper's parents' and sisters' hands and offer my condolences. When I exit the church,

I almost welcome the frigid air, as opposed to the suffocating sadness within the church.

Cooper's immediate family is going to attend his military burial at the national cemetery and then have dinner together at Cooper's favorite Italian restaurant. If Loïc were here, I'm sure I'd be going, but I can't go without him. Truthfully, they don't really know me. Maggie said I'd be welcome, but I want the family to be able to grieve among those they are close to. I'd feel like I was intruding.

It's just as well. I don't know if I can take any more sadness today.

THIRTY-SIX

London

"I love him enough to be here when he comes back to me."
—London Wright

Maggie looks well. I suppose *well* is a stretch—she looks okay. I haven't seen her in a month since the funeral. She's sitting across from me at a local café. She takes a sip of iced tea before smiling weakly.

It's a little awkward when a friendship that was built because of a common denominator—aka Cooper—attempts to continue after the mutual connection is gone. Yet I really like Maggie, and I want to keep her in my life.

"How are you doing?" I ask.

"I'm good. I mean, you know. I'll get there."

Her eyes fill with tears, and my chest aches for her.

"I'm sorry."

"I know. Me, too. It's just so surreal, you know? Most days, I can't even believe it's real. I feel like he's still deployed, and he'll come back. But he's never coming home to me." Her voice breaks along with my heart.

She absentmindedly stirs her iced tea with her straw as we sit in a heavy silence. I don't know what to say to make Maggie feel better. There's probably nothing to say.

I clear my throat. "How's work?"

"It's fine. I took a few weeks off, of course. But I've been back about two weeks now, and it's okay. I like keeping busy."

"Yeah," I agree.

"What about you? How's work?" she asks.

"Good. I've had some freelance articles printed in larger publications. I still write weekly articles for the Ann Arbor news outlet, but I'm definitely getting out there more, building my résumé."

"That's good. Still no news from Loïc?"

I shake my head. "No. I don't know what else to do. I drove out to their base in Ypsilanti the other day to see if anyone could tell me something. I practically got on my knees and begged, but they said they couldn't tell me anything. Some excuse about confidentiality or something. I'm still writing him every day, but I haven't seen him online since…" I start to say Cooper's death, but I stop myself. "You know."

"I know you'll hear from him. Loïc has always done everything on his own time. He's been through so much. I'm sure he's just taking longer to process it all. He'll come around. He loves you. He'll be back."

"Yeah, I know. I just wish he would let me help him."

"Maybe he needs to do this on his own. Everyone grieves differently."

I nod my head. "I get that. I kind of assumed that the military would let him come home early. I'm surprised that they're keeping him over there still."

"It seems weird to us, but that's the way the military is. Soldiers lose their brothers all the time over there, but they're still expected to do their job after the loss. Of course, the loss of David is more difficult for Loïc, but if you think about it, to the military, it's equivalent to the death of any brother."

"Well, I think it's stupid," I huff.

"I agree." Maggie cracks a smile, and it's so good to see her smile again. "Oh, I have news about the house. I used some of David's insurance money, that he left me in his will, to pay off the rest of the mortgage. We didn't owe much, but now, the house is all paid for. I put the deed in Loïc's name, and I moved out."

"What?"

"I just couldn't live there anymore. Too many memories." She stops talking and closes her eyes.

I want to reach across the table and hug her, but I don't know if that will help, so I stay put. It's so hard to know what to do.

She opens her eyes and lets out a pained breath of air, continuing, "I wanted Loïc to have somewhere to go when he returns. I emailed him and sent a letter, letting him know this, but of course, I haven't heard anything back."

"Where are you living now?"

"With my parents. I'll buy another house someday, but right now, it's best for me to just stay with them. They're only a fifteen-minute drive away from the hospital, and it's nice not to be alone."

"I get that. I can't believe you're not going to live there anymore though."

"I know. It sucks, but..." Her voice trails off.

"Yeah..." Sometimes, there's really nothing to say.

We finish up our lunch with only a semi-awkward conversation. Not that talking to Maggie is uncomfortable. But there's just so much we can say without causing pain to the other.

When I get back home, I open my laptop to write Loïc an email. I'm not surprised that he's not online or that he hasn't written me back. Sometimes, I feel like I'm in a relationship with myself. Part of me thinks I'm in some sort of denial—of what, I'm not sure.

I'm going to do what Maggie suggested and give him time. I love him enough to understand that he can't speak to me right now, for whatever reason. And, even though that hurts, I have to realize that he's going through something incredibly painful, and he is handling it the best he can.

I love him enough to be here when he comes back to me. And he will. He will come back to me.

THIRTY-SEVEN

London

*"There are so many variables, most of which are unknowns.
The only thing I can do is cling on to what I hold as a truth,
and that's my love for Loïc."*
—London Wright

"Honey, I'm home!" Paige calls from the back door.

"Hey, love!" I greet her from the couch where I've spent most of the day writing. "How was work?"

"Oh, great! Remember the big promotion with the online travel site?"

"Yeah, the one where they are giving away a one-thousand dollar trip voucher each day?" I recall Paige talking about it a few months ago and how bummed she was that the bitch of the office, Stephanie, got the account.

"Yes! That one. Well, Stephanie totally dropped the ball, and we almost lost the client!" she squeals, clapping her hands together.

"Uh, this is a good thing?"

"Yes, because they kicked her brown-nosing whore ass off the account and made me the new project manager! Eek!" she shrieks.

"Oh, yay!" I join in her enthusiasm.

"I know! I'm so excited. It's going to be a lot of work to clean up her mess, but if I do a great job, I'll really show my bosses what I'm capable of."

"You totally got this!"

"I know I do!" she cheers. "We totally need to celebrate! Do you feel like getting dressed today?" She quirks an eyebrow up as she eyes my yoga pants and tank top ensemble that I've been sporting since last night.

"Don't be jelly just because I don't have to get dressed for my job." I smirk.

"Oh, I'm not. But do you think you could shower real quick? I want to go somewhere fancy."

"Okay, okay. I suppose I could do that." I shoot her a wink, swinging my legs off the couch, just as my computer chimes, informing me that a new email has come in. I glance down to the screen, thinking nothing of it...until I see it's from him. "Oh my God! Oh my God! Oh my God!" I shout in rapid succession.

"What?" Paige jumps, startled.

"Loïc emailed me!" I grab my chest, sure I'm about to pass out.

"Well, what does it say?" Paige plops onto the couch beside me.

"I'm scared," I admit. My heart is seriously thrumming a painful cadence within my chest.

"It'll be okay. Just open it."

"Okay," I breathe out. "Okay."

My hand trembles as I click to open the email.

To: London Wright

From: Loïc Berkeley

Subject: Enough

It's over.

I stare at the two words contained within the email.
It's over.
What the hell?
Paige sits next to me, her gaze glued to the laptop screen containing the two vile words.

"What does that mean? He can't be referring to our relationship, can he?"

"I don't know, honestly. It's so cryptic. He could have given you a little more to go off of. Jeez," Paige huffs out.

"Maybe his tour is over? His mourning? His radio silence?"

"Dinner? His run? His shower?" Paige says, sarcasm lining her voice.

"Now is not the time for jokes. I have to figure out what he means."

"I know. I'm sorry. But, seriously." Her features scream annoyance as she shakes her head.

"Look…I get that he could have given me more. But at least he finally responded. That has to mean something."

"It's been two months since Cooper died, and he emails you two words. I'm sorry, but you deserve more than that, London."

"Thank you for being such a great friend, Paige. I appreciate you so much. Obviously, I wish things were different, but this is something at least."

"Barely."

"He's been going through a hard time. He's been through so much. He's entitled not to handle his grief well. He'll get through this. It'll be fine."

And it will be okay.

Sure, I could assume his email means the worst and break down, crumbling into a sobbing mess. But I'm not going to. I know what Loïc and I had—*have*. It is real, and it is forever. I can't pretend to know what he's going through or imagine the circumstances that caused him to write me those words.

There are so many variables, most of which are unknowns. The only thing I can do is cling on to what I hold as a truth, and that's my love for Loïc.

Unless I hear the words fall from his lips and know, without a doubt, that he means them, I won't believe them. I simply can't. Because they don't make sense.

I hate the pity I see in Paige's eyes. She looks like she's going to say something, but she only nods.

"I'm going to write him back. I'll see what he says."

I quickly write him an email.

To: Loïc Berkeley

From: London Wright

Subject: I love you.

Loïc,

I don't understand what your email means.

We need to talk. I can't imagine what you're going through, but I want to help.

I know that we can get through anything—even this, as long as we're together.

I will never give up on you or us. Please, talk to me. Call me, anytime.

I love you so very much.

Love,

London

I wait a minute after clicking *send*. When he doesn't respond right away, I close down the laptop. "All right, Paigey Poo, let's go celebrate you."

THIRTY-EIGHT

London

*"What the heart knows and what it chooses to believe
are two different things."*
—London Wright

I sprint out into the living room to find Paige sprawled
on the couch, reading a magazine.

"Maggie just texted me!" I shriek, causing Paige to
toss the magazine up with a yelp.

"Say it; don't scream it. Jeez, London," Paige says,
holding a hand to her chest.

"Sorry." I shake my head. "But she said that Loïc is
back and that I should go over and see him."

"Really?" Paige quickly sits up. "Well, go. What are
you waiting for?"

"I don't know!" I cry as I jump up and down,
clapping my hands. "What should I wear? What should I
say? Oh my gosh!"

"You look fine. Just go. Oh, but I'd at least brush your teeth. You know what they say. *Actions speak louder than words.*"

"Of course I'll brush my teeth. I haven't kissed him in months. Our first kiss is going to be minty fresh." I practically skip into my room.

Within five minutes, I'm in my car, driving toward Loïc's house in Ypsilanti. I can't believe that I'm about to see him. He's been gone almost exactly five months, but it feels like an eternity, especially the last two months. I haven't heard from him since his cryptic two-worded email last week. So, maybe he meant that his tour was over, that he was coming home. I just don't understand why he couldn't call or write with more information.

But I'm not going to let myself go there. He's here. He's home, and I'm about to see him. That's more than I could have hoped for. The rest, we'll figure out.

I pull into his driveway, parking behind his truck. There's another car in the drive that I don't recognize. At first, I think that maybe Maggie got a different car and that she's here, visiting, until I remember that she had to work tonight.

She must have been here earlier anyway. *How else would she have known that Loïc was back?*

It's strange that Maggie no longer lives here, but I don't blame her. I can't imagine how difficult it would be for her to stay in her and Cooper's home.

I exit my car, and the May sun warms my skin, wrapping me in a blanket of hope. I pull in a deep breath, inhaling *life*—freshly cut grass, blossoming lilacs from a nearby bush, recent rain, and soil from the earth. I'm surrounded by new beginnings, and finally, after months of doubt and coldness, I know it's going to be okay.

I'm about to see Loïc.

Jogging up the front porch steps, I'm suddenly overcome by a nervous energy. *Why didn't Loïc tell me that he was back?* I push that thought away as I knock on the door. *It doesn't matter because I'm seconds away from seeing him, and then everything will be right again.*

I wait for what seems like forever before knocking again.

Finally, I hear someone unlock the door. When it swings open, I'm not face-to-face with Loïc but Sarah, and as I scan down her body—

Her stomach.

My eyes bulge at the sight of her very pregnant belly.

"London!" Sarah exclaims, sounding shocked. "What are you doing here?" The question isn't asked in a rude tone, but at the same time, I can't believe she just asked me that.

"To see Loïc."

I have to stop myself from saying, *Duh*, afterward. Sarah has this way of bringing out the worst in me.

"Oh, right. Well, um…you can't see him right now," she finally stammers out.

My mouth opens wide in a gasp. She's standing on the other side of the screen door in tight black leggings and an itty-bitty tank top that barely contains her Hooters boobs. Even with a watermelon belly, she's hotter than most women I know. I hate her.

"What do you mean, I can't see him right now? Sarah, I want to see Loïc," I snap.

"I'm sorry, London." She looks down before her gaze catches mine, and she continues, "He doesn't want to see you. I'm sorry."

"That's ridiculous. Please go tell him I am here. Tell him that I need to see him. You can't keep him from me," I bite out.

"Hold on," she sighs. She has the audacity to look remorseful before she shuts the door in my face.

You've got to be kidding me.

A minute later, the door opens.

"He says he doesn't want to see you and to please go. I'm sorry." Sarah gives me a faint smile.

"I don't care what you say. I'm not leaving here until I see my boyfriend."

"But he broke up with you," she says bluntly.

What?

Yes, I know she's referring to the email, and in my heart, I've known all along that was his intention, but he didn't mean it. I know he didn't.

"It was two words in an email. That hardly counts as a breakup," I growl at the tall, busty blonde in front of me.

"Well, I think it does to him, so you need to accept it."

"What are you doing here anyway?" I'm being so rude, but I couldn't care less. I have one objective, and that's to see Loïc. The fact that she's stopping me is really pissing me off.

"I live here—with Loïc."

That bitch just threw those last two words in to piss me off.

"Why?"

"Because he wants me here. Because I want to. We're going to raise the baby here."

And there you have it.

That one little word is like a freezing waterfall extinguishing my small candle.

Baby.

A second ago, I would have knocked this bitch down to get to Loïc, but that word completely doused my fire. In the blink of an eye, I lost my fight.

Baby.

She and Loïc are going to raise a baby? What is happening here? Will someone please bring me back to reality?

I'm standing motionless on the porch. Who knows what expression my face wears, but I'm sure it's disturbing. My chest aches, and I struggle to find air. It's so cold, and I strive to feel the comforting spring day, but I can't.

I don't understand what's going on.

I just need Loïc.

Sarah presses her lips into a line before saying, "Good-bye, London."

Then, she closes the door on me. The lock turns, and I'm still here.

This isn't real.

Nothing makes sense.

I gasp, the harsh breath bringing life to my lungs. I stare at the closed door a second longer before finally grasping enough sense to walk back to my car.

I don't even remember the drive back to my house. Yet I'm now walking up to my front door.

I can't even cry. I can't even mourn this. Whatever this is, it isn't my life.

This is not how things go down.

This is not how things end.

My front door opens with a whoosh.

"What are you doing out here? What's wrong?" Paige asks. "You've been standing out here for at least five minutes."

I follow Paige inside and plop down on the couch, still unable to formalize a thought. I'm in shock.

"London, you need to start talking. You're scaring me. Did you see him?" She paces in front of me. "Did you see Loïc?"

I raise my head at the sound of his name, and I meet Paige's concerned stare. "No." I shake my head. "They're raising a baby. She's pregnant," I stammer out.

"Who?"

"I saw Sarah. She's pregnant. She wouldn't let me see him. She said he didn't want to see me."

"Loïc and Sarah are having a baby? He cheated on you?" Paige shrieks.

"No, he wouldn't." My words come out slowly.

Paige snaps her fingers in front of my face. "Earth to London. Snap out of it, love. I need to know everything."

"That's all really. She said I couldn't see him. I was fighting her on it, but then she talked about them raising a baby together, and I kind of had an internal freak-out, I think."

"How big is her belly?"

"What?"

"How big is it?" Paige urges.

"I don't know. Big."

"Well, the last time she saw Loïc was the first week of December when she drove up to surprise him before the guys left, remember? That was five months ago, like exactly. Does she look five months pregnant?"

"I don't know, Paige. Her belly's big." I sigh.

"Yeah, well, that doesn't mean anything. Women carry differently. She's so skinny. Maybe she looks further along than she is, you know? I've known people with good-sized bellies at five months."

"No." I shake my head. "He wouldn't have cheated on me."

"How do you know? He broke up with you over an email. I don't think you know him as well as you think you do."

"I know him," I protest. "The email said, *It's over.* That could mean anything. Maybe his deployment is over? His mourning period for Cooper? Who knows?" I know, in my heart…I do. But what the heart knows and what it chooses to believe are two different things.

"London, you're being naive."

"No, I'm not. You don't know Loïc like I do. He wouldn't cheat on me. He loves me. Something's wrong. I don't know what happened over there, but he needs me. He's probably depressed because Cooper died. Plus, who knows what else he saw? I'm not giving up on him. I won't. Something doesn't add up. Maybe he needs time? Or perhaps I just have to be more persistent. I'm not going to let that blonde bitch keep me from him. I know that, once he sees me and we can be together and talk things through, then it will be okay. We'll be okay," I say, reassuring myself more than anything.

Paige sits next to me. Her lips press into a sad line. She tucks a loose piece of my hair behind my ears and stares at me. I don't like the pity I see in her eyes.

"London, you know that saying? *If you love something, set it free. If it comes back, it is yours. If it doesn't, it never was.* Maybe you need to move on and put the ball in Loïc's court."

I adamantly shake my head. "No, that doesn't apply here at all. That's a horrible suggestion."

"London…" Concern lines Paige's voice.

"Stop. I know what you're thinking. I'm not weak. If I thought that Loïc had the capacity to cheat on me, then I'd be reacting differently. Yes, the baby thing threw me off-balance for a hot second…but I'm back. I'm telling you, something's not right. Maybe Sarah's lying, or maybe Loïc's just helping her because she has no one else. I'm not sure, but I'll find out," I say with conviction.

"All right, but as your best friend, I need to say this, and I need you to hear it. You can choose what to do with it after that, but please at least just listen. Okay?"

"Say what you need to say," I groan, expelling a breath.

She places a hand on my leg. "Loïc is the first man you've ever been in love with, and I know you love him a lot. I think you love him so much that you can't imagine your life without him. I know your love is real. But you can't judge *his* feelings based off of yours. No matter how much you love someone, you can't make him love you the same unless he wants to. I believe you're in denial, and I think the longer it takes you to figure that out, the harder it's going to be when you do. I know you're going to be heartbroken. But you have to let him go, so you can heal and move on."

I place my hand on top of hers. "I'm so thankful that I have someone like you who loves me so much. I love you, Paigey Poo. But you're wrong about Loïc, and I'm going to prove it. I'm going to get him back."

I smile wide and hop off the couch. I need to go call Georgia with the recent developments and start working on my plan.

Denial, my ass.

I get what I want...especially when what I want is the love of my life.

Loïc might not know it, but he wants that, too.

THIRTY-NINE

Loïc

"When the mind is weak, nothing else matters."
—Loïc Berkeley

My phone buzzes with another text from London.

I love you. Forever. Please call me.

I can't take much more of her constant texting and calling. Each time she calls, I want to throw away my phone for good. I especially can't handle when she stops by and pounds on my door for what seems like hours. I can't risk seeing her. I feel like a prisoner in my own home—for more reasons than one.

I wish I could just get rid of my phone altogether. I don't want one. I wouldn't need one either, except to talk to Maggie. I have to have a way for Maggie to get ahold of me. She calls fairly regularly—most times, late at night, when she's crying. I always pick up. She deserves that. Cooper deserves that. I think it helps Maggie grieve to talk to me partly because I was close to Cooper, too, and partly because I was with him when he died.

I'm leaning back in a lawn chair in our backyard. It's a seemingly perfect May day in Michigan. A warm breeze moves across my skin. I would normally be out kayaking or hiking. But I can't do any of that. I can't find a sliver of joy among my darkness.

"Hey, babycakes," a very cheerful Sarah stands beside me, casting a shadow over my chest.

"Hi."

"The baby's kicking. Do you want to feel him?" she asks excitedly, bending to grab my hand before I've answered.

She places my open palm against her belly, and the two of us wait in silence. After a few beats, he kicks.

"Did you feel it?" she shrieks.

"Yeah, I did."

"Isn't that awesome? He's so strong."

I nod. "He is."

"We need to talk more about the names. Have you thought of any good ones?"

"I told you, Sarah, that's your call. Name him whatever you want."

"But I want your help," she whines.

"Well, I can't think of any."

"We should go somewhere today," she says, changing the subject. "Where do you want to go? It's so gorgeous out!" she exclaims brightly, holding her face up to the sun.

"I don't feel like going anywhere."

She plops down in the grass beside me. "Tell me a story of London, of your nan and granddad."

"Not today."

She continues, as if she didn't hear me, "Remember how many stories you used to tell me of your childhood? You had so many. Do you still remember them all? Or we could play I Spy. We used to play that game all the time. I think your game and stories single-handedly stopped us from going crazy of boredom every night." She laughs to herself. More quietly, she adds, "It's weird that I had some of the best times of my life when I was homeless with you, you know?"

"Yeah, I do."

"Look at us now. We've come a long way since those days." Sighing happily, she asks, "Can I get you anything? A sandwich? A glass of lemonade? I just made some."

"Okay, a lemonade."

"Great," she says, standing. She squats down and smooths my hair away from my forehead before planting a quick kiss there. "You know, we're going to be okay. You're going to be okay, Loïc. I will never leave you. I will always be here for you."

"I know." I nod.

She smiles before standing again and heading into the house.

She's such a ray of sunshine in my life, but I struggle to feel her warmth. I'm having a hard time with life right now, and I know Sarah is trying to make it better.

Yet, each time I look at her, I feel anxious. I can't let down anyone else in my life. Truthfully, it'd be easier for me to have no real relationships. I think I was right about that from a young age. Relationships lead to love, and love leads to loss. Every. Single. Time.

I can't cut Sarah out though. I feel a strong sense of obligation to her. I always have but especially now.

I'm just so tired. I'm walking around blind in a world that doesn't make sense.

There's no light because I can't break out of this perpetual night that I'm in. My mind holds dark thoughts, horribly gruesome visions, that I have no ability to control.

When one thinks about a warrior, they think of a strong person who has the capacity to yield something powerful. But what everyone fails to realize is that the mind is the biggest muscle of them all. The brain controls everything. When the mind is weak, nothing else matters. When the mind is fragile, one is left helpless.

I'm fighting to find purpose. I'm trying to find a point to it all or at least a semblance of peace. Yet, right now, all I feel is hopelessness.

My dad was wrong. I'm no warrior. I'm a weak-minded coward. Perhaps I always was.

FORTY

London

"I more than love him. The way I feel about Loïc is more than just a need, a want, a feeling. It's more than a word."
—London Wright

Paige and I are doing a *Friends* marathon on Netflix. This show reminds me of my mom. She bought all the seasons on DVD when I was younger, and she, Georgia, and I spent an entire week one summer watching every single episode from all ten seasons. This show somehow seems timeless to me. I just love it. Every couple of years, I do a marathon. I keep hoping to see the news come out that they're going to make a *Friends* movie to update us on their current lives. Yet, so far, nothing.

"Oh my God...this is the best part." Paige chuckles as Ross's boss arrives to visit him at his new apartment after Ross's mandatory time off from going crazy at work, right after his second marriage—the one with Emily—failed.

"He's hilarious," I agree though my voice sounds dull and way less enthusiastic than it should be.

It was Paige's idea to do a *Friends* marathon. I'm sure she thought some comedy could get me out of my funk. I wish it were that easy.

A marginal smile crosses my face as I think of the scene about to happen. Ross is my favorite. Everyone on the show is hysterical, but there is something about him that cracks me up every time. He's so out there that it's funny. From his apartment window, he's about to see Monica and Chandler having sex in her apartment, and he's going to totally lose it in front of his boss. Normally, I'd already be in tears from laughter.

But the laughter isn't coming, and God knows, I don't need any more tears.

Just as Ross's eyes bulge and he starts yelling for Chandler to get off his sister, my phone buzzes next to me on the couch.

I glance down and see Loïc's name come up on my screen. "Stop it! Stop it!" I shout to Paige as I point to the TV. "It's him!"

She quickly pauses the show and looks at me, wide-eyed and expectant.

"What do I do?" I ask her.

"Pick it up," she urges.

The phone buzzes for the third time. "I don't know. What do I say…" My thoughts are a jumbled mess as I plead to Paige for an answer to a question I've yet to ask.

I've waited so long for him to call me. I've dreamed about hearing his voice again. Now, he's calling.

My body floods with equal parts fear and relief, but both of them are drowning in my sea of panic.

What does he want? He must be ready to talk? Does he miss me? Does he want to get back together? Is he calling to tell me that he's sorry for putting me through this heartache? Maybe he's calling to tell me he's on his way over? Does he want to talk about the baby and reassure me that it isn't his?

It can't be his.

Paige shouts, "London! Pick it up!"

I jump, startled.

I quickly slide the screen to accept the call before it goes to voice mail and then slowly bring the phone to my ear. "Hello?" My voice is weak and shaky, but nonetheless, it sounds stronger than I feel.

"It's me," he says quietly in a voice that's low and hollow.

I barely recognize the sound of him, but it's him.

My heart beats wildly in my chest. "Hi." I pull in a deep breath. "I'm so glad you called."

"Listen, London, you have to stop this."

His comment confuses me.

"What?"

"You have to stop calling and texting. You can't come over here again. It's over, London," he says with authority before pausing. I hear him sigh. "Okay? It's over." This time, he sounds less sure.

"But—"

He cuts me off, "No, London. But nothing. It's over. I can't keep doing this with you."

Loïc's good-bye sets a fire to my soul, giving me a renewed sense of strength.

This will not be it. He cannot do this to me, to us. He's confused or scared. I have to prove to him that he's wrong.

"Loïc, I need to see you. We need to talk. Whatever is going on…let me help you. We can work on this together. It's not over. Please let me in. I love you." My voice breaks on the last sentence. Those three little words don't even do justice to the way I feel about him.

I more than love him. The way I feel about Loïc is more than just a need, a want, a feeling. It's more than a word. It's a lifetime of commitment. It's a lifetime of love, respect, trust. It's an eternity of hugs, laughter, passion, and lust. It's everything I say and do forever. Loïc will be present in every thought and action I take for the rest of my life.

Yes, I more than love Loïc. I *live* him. With every heartbeat, every breath, and every thought, I live him. And he will be a part of me for the rest of my life.

"London, I'm fucked up." His voice is pained, so desolate and sad.

My chest aches, and I long to hold him.

I inhale, pulling another breath into my lungs, before saying, "It's okay. Remember...we can be fucked up together? We can get through anything if we're together. I can help you. I can love you like no one else ever can. We are meant to be together, Loïc. There is no one else on this earth for me. You are it. I'm yours, and you're mine."

"I don't believe in that."

"Well, I believe enough for the both of us," I reassure him.

"You see, my heart and its capacity to love is my biggest flaw of all. I warned you, London. I told you this would happen."

"What?"

"From the very beginning, I told you that I would hurt you. I wouldn't want to, but I would. I told you that I lose everything I love. I warned you. I begged you to stay away." His deep timbre cracks on the last word.

"You haven't lost me. You'll never lose me. And your heart's not flawed. I know you, Loïc. Just come over.

Let's talk. Everything will be better once we're together. I promise you."

"It's over, London. We're over. Please let me go." His plea is so desperate, his voice so raw.

Tears course down my cheeks. "We're not. Please. It will be okay."

"We're over," he says once more. "I'm sorry."

"But…no," I cry out in despair.

"London, you're hurting me. You. Are. Hurting. Me."

I suck in a breath at his harsh words.

"Please…*please*…let me go," he begs.

His voice radiates with a pain I've never known. It's a sorrow so tangible that it hits me through the phone, weighing down on me like a mountain of tears.

I struggle to breathe. "Loïc," I cry, sobbing now.

"Please, let me go. Just let me go," he whispers before the line goes dead.

I'm left clutching the phone to my ear, desperately clinging to the need to hear a voice I'm afraid I'll never hear again.

I rock back and forth on the couch as sobs rack my body. Every inch of me mourns the loss of Loïc. I cradle the phone against my chest and hug it as the tears continue to fall in streams, physical manifestations of the immense amount of anguish needing to leave my body. I'm filled with too much grief to bear. I have to ease the stress on my soul, or it will suffocate me.

I cry until my head throbs with pain. I sit up from my hunched rocking position, and it's only then that I notice Paige is sitting next to me. Her face is wet with tears. She pulls me into her chest, and I hug her tight, grateful for the comfort of someone who loves me.

She doesn't say anything as she rubs my back, the gesture calming.

I sit up and look to her. "What is it that they always say?" I question sadly. "If you love someone, set them free?"

She nods weakly, her eyes filling with tears. "Yeah," she sighs. "That's what they say."

"I have to let him go, Paige," I choke out, unable to believe the words coming from my mouth even though I know them to be true.

"Yeah"—a tear falls down her cheek—"I think so."

Because I love Loïc with everything that I am, I have to respect his wishes. Somehow, someway…I have to.

If you love someone, set them free.
If you love someone…

Set.

Them.

Free.

LOVING LONDON

BOOK THREE IN THE FLAWED HEART SERIES

COMING SOON

ACKNOWLEDGMENTS

This series holds a special place in my heart. I just adore London and Loïc! I hope you enjoyed reading this complex and heartbreaking chapter of their journey.

The next book, Loving London, will be the final book in this series and it's going to give you all sorts of feels, just as I'm sure this one did! I can't wait for you to have London and Loïc's complete story in your hands.

It is so crazy to me that I am publishing my seventh book, and what makes it more surreal is the fact that I'm doing it as a full-time writer! This is no longer my hobby but my legit job—the best job. I never thought I would be sitting here, saying this, yet here I am, people! Amazing. Dreams do come true! ☺ What a gift. ♥

I want to thank my readers so very much. Thank you for reading my stories and loving my words! I wouldn't be living this dream without you. Thank you from the bottom of my heart!

In every one of my acknowledgment sections, I get quite wordy when expressing my love to all the amazing people in my life. I am so fortunate to have this life I've been given. I have a wonderful husband, healthy and happy children, an astonishing extended family, the best mother in the world, and friends who would do anything for me. I am so blessed and grateful to be surrounded by so much love that I want to shout it from the rooftops.

For this book especially I want to thank Lt. Col. Ryan Ismirle of the United States Airforce. I appreciate you being available for my numerous questions about serving in Afghanistan and basically everything military related. I appreciate your help in making this story as authentic as possible. Thank you so much for your service to our amazing country.

A special shout-out will always go to my siblings, who were my first soul mates. You will find them in every story I write because so much of what I know of love has come from them. One of my biggest wishes for my children is that they will always love each other unconditionally and fiercely, the way my siblings and I love each other.

There is a core group of people who go above and beyond in helping me with my books—most of whom, I didn't know prior to becoming a part of this crazy book world—and I am so thankful.

To my beta readers and proofreaders—Gayla, Nicole, Amy, Tammi, Elle, Heather, Terri, and Angela—You all are so awesome. Seriously, each of you is a gift, and you have helped me in invaluable different ways. I love you all so much. XOXO

Angela, my cupcake—I've said it before, and I will say it again. I love you big time, like hard-core, intense love! I am counting down the days until we meet in person! I can't thank you enough for all you do for me on a daily basis! I am so truly blessed to know you. ♥

Gayla—Thank you for taking time out of your busy life to help me, no matter what I need. You are so smart and talented. You are a blessing, and I love you more than I could ever express.

Nicole, my BBWFL—You are my biggest supporter and ally in this crazy book world. You will always get the credit for starting it all. Our mutual love of books and our late-night chats reignited my dream to write. None of my books would be the same without your input. Your friendship means the world to me. Love you forever.

Tammi—I've said it before, and I will say it again. I will forever continue to write as long as you continue to read because your feedback alone is enough. *You get me.* Thank you for being you because you are perfect. I live for your comments and feedback. Not only do you fill my heart with so much gratitude, but you also make me a better writer. *Tight Hugs* I freaking love you!

Amy, my BBFFL—What can I say that I haven't already said? You know how much I love you! I have cherished your support from the beginning. Six novels later, you continue to bless me with your feedback and support. You get me and my writing. You make my books better. You are one of the kindest and most supportive people I know. I love you to pieces! ♥

Terri—I'm still so grateful that I met you and thankful that you continue to beta! You know exactly how to make my work better. Thank you for your honest feedback. You are such a kind, smart, and giving person. I hope you know that, now that I've found you, I'm not going to let you go! ☺ XO

Elle—I love you for so many reasons! I especially love how you make me laugh when I need it! Thank you for loving and supporting me. You are such a good person. Thank you for all you do to help me! I am so grateful. ♥

To my cover artist, Regina Wamba from Mae I Design and Photography—Thank you! Your work inspires me. You are a true artist, and I am so grateful to now have seven of your covers. People do judge a book by its cover, so thank you for making mine *gorgeous*! XO

To my editor and interior designer, Jovana Shirley from Unforeseen Editing—You are, simply put, the best. Your talent, professionalism, and the care you take with my novels are worth way more than I could ever afford to pay you. Finding you was a true gift, one that I hope to always have on this journey. Thank you from the bottom of my heart for not only making my words pretty, but for also making the interior of the book beautiful. Thank you for always fitting me in! I am so grateful for you and everything you have done to make this book the best it can be. XOXO

Lastly, to the bloggers—Oh my God! I love you! Since releasing *Forever Baby*, I have gotten to know many of you through Facebook. Out of the kindness of your hearts, so many of you have reached out and helped me promote my books. There are seriously great people in this blogger community, and I am humbled by your support. Truly, thank you! Because of you, indie authors get their stories out. Thank you for supporting all authors and the great stories they write.

Readers—You can connect with me on several places, and I would love to hear from you.

Find me on Facebook:
www.facebook.com/EllieWadeAuthor

Find me on Twitter: @authorelliewade

Visit my website: www.elliewade.com

Remember, the greatest gift you can give an author is a review. If you feel so inclined, please leave a review on the various retailer sites. It doesn't have to be fancy. A couple of sentences would be awesome!

I could honestly write a whole book about everyone in this world whom I am thankful for. I am blessed in so many ways, and I am beyond grateful for this beautiful life. XOXO

Forever,

Ellie ❤

ABOUT THE AUTHOR

Ellie Wade resides in southeast Michigan with her husband, three young children, and two dogs. She has a master's in education from Eastern Michigan University, and she is a huge University of Michigan sports fan. She loves the beauty of her home state, especially the lakes and the gorgeous autumn weather. When she is not writing, she is reading, snuggling up with her kids, or spending time with family and friends. She loves traveling and exploring new places with her family.

Made in the USA
Middletown, DE
28 July 2024